SHOULD HAVE BEEN

LAKE SPARK INN

BOOK 3

EVEY LYON

SUMMER

This isn't the way it was supposed to be.

That's what I think, as my feet dangling over the lake water as I sit on the edge of the dock. This spot to perch is only fitting. It reminds me of *that summer*, after all.

The summer where I was stuck in a corner between the Nix brothers. Zac, my closest friend, who was without a clue that his brother Nash was more.

And here I am seven years later after having my heart broken… twice. But broken in two very different ways. That's what the Nix brothers do to a human. Or at least me.

The two brothers were always complete opposites. Zac was slim and not as tall, still attractive to most, even if he often had his nose in a book, whereas Nash was and still is the guy who has a bit of muscle and a look that is cocky and tense. His glances could slice the air in half, if that were possible. Maybe that's why hockey was his calling. He was Zac's Irish twin, only ten months older. But old enough for Nash to go into protective big-brother mode, which was my undoing.

Now my husband is gone.

Zac Nix is gone.

Our marriage wasn't what it seemed, but we cared for one another all the same, and we created a child from our hearts, which means I'll always have a piece of him. A ping hits my heart. He left us five months ago, and now I have a seven-month-old baby.

Cancer is a bitch, and the path he left behind wanders around corners too sharp.

Luckily, footsteps break my morbid thoughts.

"Hey, Summer, I saw you from the window by the lobby," my friend Lexi informs me.

I glance over my shoulder to be greeted with a smile and the backdrop of the Dizzy Duck Inn. The place where people escape Chicago for a weekend getaway. Even now, when the leaves begin to turn and the charm of lake swims and sailing fade away.

"Hey." My tone must sound somber to her.

She drags her shiny blonde locks up into a messy ponytail and sits down next to me.

Lexi nudges my shoulder. "Big day."

It causes a crack of a smile to break out. "No shit. I've had my playlist on repeat for the past three hours while I was handling payroll in the staffroom. How is the lookout going?"

She winces. "Sorry. I'm not on my A-game with my detective skills today. School drop-off was an adventure this morning. Holden and Lori might kill one another soon." A fond smile hits her face.

She's perfect for Holden, who runs the Dizzy Duck Inn, and Lexi is perfect as a stepmom too, even if the school moms get snooty at her for the age difference. I can only imagine that rearing a thirteen-year-old and an eleven-year-old doesn't come easy.

I give her an amused look. "Did we not establish that today we have priorities? Holden can deal with teenage angst for the team. I needed you to be Sherlock today."

"Well, you already know…" She's dreading to remind me.

I wave her off. "That he checked in? Yeah, I heard someone mention. But damn it, I need more clues or at least a giant bucket of ice cream from Jolly Joe's."

"Gosh, our local Lake Spark establishment never fails us. Cures everything. Did you hear the bubble gum ice cream is back?"

My nose squinches. "Disgusting. If I want bubble gum flavor, then I'll just grab the children's medicine from the pharmacy," I attempt to joke.

"I know, right?" I appreciate her effort to distract me.

This is a big day. My entire body is unsettled, and my heart isn't ready for this either.

Zac, a doctor, so meticulous, left behind a house that's mine, a child so perfect, and assurance that my support network of friends won't leave me to be alone. He also passed on without ever learning of the secret I carried.

I focus my gaze on the pines surrounding the other side of the serene lake. Blowing out a breath, I can't keep it in anymore. "Tell me I'm not heading toward a car crash that I've already been in?"

Lexi opens her mouth, a sound scraping out, only to close her lips as she considers her answer. "I'm sure it's fine. Everyone needs a former hockey star to argue with. Besides, Nash is Bo's uncle."

I laugh to myself. "Really? Could have fooled me. Nash Nix has a shitty way of showing it."

"Want me to come over later, see how it all goes?" she offers.

"Nah, I have a new bottle of white in my fridge. We're good. Besides it's almost twelve, so no need to doubt when to open the bottle." I don't even really drink except for the occasional dinner. But desperate times, desperate measures, right?

Lexi rubs my shoulder. "Good philosophy to have. You've got this."

"Thanks." My voice thins.

She begins to scurry up to leave me. "If you need anything at all, just send me an SOS."

"Will do." I sigh.

My eyes shift down to the ripples in the water beneath my sneakered feet; there must have been a tiny fish that jumped. As a kid, I would imagine there were pirates on the lake, with treasure along the bottom. A ridiculous notion considering we aren't far from the corn fields that surround us, once you escape the hills surrounding the lake. I only ever shared that secret with one person, and I'm not sure why. We shared many secrets, actually.

Some more earth-shattering than others.

And now that man is walking around Lake Spark.

Okay, find another thought, Summer.

My job. Yes, my job. I love my job managing the staff at the Dizzy Duck Inn. Brings me joy, and damn, the stories of what happens there can make anyone grab a seat and wish they could watch while eating popcorn. Thanks to Holden, I get to work around my schedule, too. Which has been a saving grace when balancing a baby and mourning a loss, even though I'm finding normalcy again.

This doesn't seem to detour the pit in my stomach.

Nash.

Occasionally, Nash would sweep into our life, or rather Zac's, at random moments, and despite time passing, they always picked up where they left off. Nash was so busy with his hockey life, after all. I scoff, because for someone who is all steely and confident on the ice, he avoids me or any situation where he had to face Zac and me as a couple. If our eyes ever met, then he would only take a few moments before he would ensure his eyes snapped in a new direction.

Damn it, Zac. What have you done? Leaving me.

Because I already feel the dread and fear, purely for the fact that Nash is in Lake Spark today to speak with Zac's lawyer about his testament. The part of his will that I have no clue the contents.

I've handled Zac's death well for the most part. Despite the anger he caused in me that I don't want to think about now, we had the chance to say goodbye, and he was insistent that it shouldn't be a sad moment. He promised to be winking at me from up in the sky. But I can't help feeling that he didn't tell me something.

He was a good soul, so kind and fun, but sometimes he would be lost in thought when Nash's name was mentioned, because he missed his tight bond with his brother that they once had.

Shit. Younger us really fucked up life slightly.

My nails begin to tap the wood that I'm sitting on. There is no way to sweep away the image of where Nash is right now. Probably strolling on Main Street, with the baking club ladies sitting on a bench all ogle-eyed. I bet he's flashing them a suave grin to rile them up. Right before his eyes catch sight of the new nurse in town that might be of interest, and the mere thought causes a cold shiver to run down my spine.

Summer, come on. Get it together. You have moved on like a storm heading east.

But then I feel him before I even hear the soft steps. My body stiffens, and I'm too late to take a calming breath.

My body feels like I've eaten a hot tamale, and I climb up

to face Nash who takes over my vision. His gleaming brown eyes and his face with short stubble are unreadable, but it's still damaging. The maroon t-shirt hugs the curves of his broad shoulders, and his light brown hair is short as always.

Our eyes meet in a tense standoff, and words lodge in my throat. Nash doesn't bother examining any other part of my body because his piercing eyes have trapped me.

"Did you find your treasure yet?" That deep voice wraps around me.

I may fear him because it's due to him that I have a different path in life. And despite nearly hating this man… my heart thrums.

NASH

"Well?" Summer finally manages to say.

Those are her first words? No hello?

Summer's eyes blaze open, and a thin line draws on her lips that are a shade of pink with a glaze of lip balm. Realizing that I'm glancing at her lips, I snap my sight up to study her brown eyes and the way her dark blonde hair forms a trail around her face, hiding the small scar on her forehead.

Shaking my need to soak in the image of her and the fact my chest constricts, I stay firm in my stance and decide to get right to it. Where do we pick up, anyhow? "I met with the lawyer."

"No shit. Not really news." Sass? That's the emotion she's choosing to give me right now?

But it causes the corner of my mouth to tug slightly from amusement. "I've been made executor of Zac's will." The document that we were told to wait to open.

It should have been an old game collection he left me or asking me to put money aside for Bo's college fund. Or he could've left me his stocks, but my brother always had thoughts that he kept to himself. It's just the logic behind this request that has me muddled, with no clear reasoning in my brain.

Summer stands tall, with her arms crossed around her chest, and with that t-shirt, it causes her breasts to lift, which I notice because I'm apparently an immoral person when it comes to this situation.

Creases form between her brows. "He never shared that with me."

I nod subtly once and swallow because the start of our rollercoaster of what-the-fuck moments is about to begin. "And also..."

She gawks at me. "Care to elaborate?" Summer has her feisty A-game on today.

"He requested that I move in... with you... for six weeks."

Her body completely freezes.

She's shocked, and quite frankly, so am I. This is not the news I imagined I would be delivering today.

A croak escapes Summer's throat as her mouth cracks open; she seems to be digesting the news.

"No," she states firmly her delayed response to my bombshell.

"Yes," I sigh.

"No," she repeats.

"Yes," I volley back.

Look at us, already quarrelling. She throws her hands up into the air. "Why the hell would he request that?"

I scan the area and wonder why it is so quiet today at the Dizzy Duck. I should probably take more interest in my tiny investment. My parents sold off the Dizzy Duck under the contingency that a small part was kept in the family. Since Zac had no interest, I kept 10%. Two other hockey guys completely took over the place, and I already knew them well enough.

Pinching my nose, I'm reminded that the only route of escape is turning my back on Summer. I mean, maybe jumping on a rowboat could be an option, but that seems kind of extreme. Hesitantly, I take a few steps in her direction to close our distance. Closer is my undoing around her.

"It's his request," I recap.

"I'll contest it," she says tightly.

I glide my tongue along my inner cheek, doing my best to stay calm. "Really? Of all the things, that's what you want to waste your time on? You know your desire to honor his wishes will only stop you from picking up the phone to call a lawyer anyhow."

Summer rolls her eyes while her shoulders drop, knowing damn well I'm right. "Are you going to follow it?"

Scratching the back of my neck, I go over the thoughts I had running through my head on the drive over. Zac was my little brother; I always felt a protective nature over him, but now he has asked me to take care of what he held so precious and close to his heart.

But it's Summer…

"My hockey career finished a year ago," I highlight.

I never played for the Spinners, the team that practices here in town, my career mostly took me to Michigan. Not to say I haven't spent many hours on the ice here in Lake Spark. "Besides, I have a tiny stake in the inn, too."

She chirps a laugh. "Now you want to take interest in the inn? That's rich, considering you didn't seem to have a lot of time for your family before."

I step forward, feeling a charge of regret and anger. "That's not true," I defend. But I'm not sure why I'm attempting. I've been a little more than absent over the past few years.

Summer stands with her hands in fists hanging at her sides. "Really? At the funeral you hid in the back. When Bo was born, you didn't even visit." Nor could I watch Zac and Summer together after they eloped or while they held their son together. "Just like you didn't when Zac was sick. How many times did you visit him then?"

My palm soars up to calm her. "More than you realize. Damn, Summer, you know I saw him a few times in private."

Just not enough.

She scoffs at me. "Away from my watch, right?" Her voice is soft and subdued, her eyes dropping low.

A long silence floats in the air as we both relay the facts of history in our head.

"He loved you." More than I could, or at least that's what I tell myself to dull the pain.

She strikes her glance up to me with tears pooling in her eyes. "He did love me, and I loved him… but you know it's not…" She hesitates doesn't finish her sentence.

It's Summer. She and Zac were close friends since they were probably thirteen. She always looked out for him when they were teenagers. And for that, she held a high position in our hearts.

In high school, she ignored social hierarchy and was kind to everyone. Zac had been sick, in and out of the hospital for cancer treatment more times than I care to count, and every single time she showed up with the right movie or care package to make him happy. They were always friends, until recently.

The only thing Summer has ever done wrong is…

Stopping myself, I divert my thoughts away from facts that nobody knows except her.

"We're both in a situation we never planned on. You're a widow now and—"

"Don't you dare say it, Nash." She walks past me, and I follow her trail before she turns back to me, frustrated. "What? Am I not playing the part of a grieving widow enough? Do I look like someone who needs a man to sweep in and save her?"

I bring my hand to my hip while I swipe the other across my stubbled jaw. "It's his request," I reiterate.

Way to go, Nash, saying that for the thousandth time.

"You were his wife, he… I also spoke with my mom."

She eases a smidgen. "I'm in contact with Walter and Gail, update them a few times a week via text about Bo. I guess they need space to mourn, and that's why they're staying at their vacation house in North Carolina."

My lips twitch from the fact that they are hurting, too. Zac, the favorite son. They always had a better relationship with him, I can't deny that. "They want to stay there for a change of scene, and they've decided to sell their house here and want me to handle that." Her mouth forms an O shape. "And… they are worried about you. You're alone in taking care of their grandson."

Her sound of anger hits my ears at record speed. "Don't," she barks out. "They wouldn't try to take him from me, would they?"

I'm quick to clarify. "Absolutely not. It's just… they also want me to ensure that you and Bo are okay."

She tosses her arms up in the air. "Can everyone in your family get a grip? My family too. My brother checks in nearly every day in place of my parents who are always MIA. I'm fine, not made of glass. I've mourned, and I refuse to feel guilty for finding a routine again."

It's a long pause because I'm mulling over if I believe her.

"They care. I ca— Watching out for you is what your husband would have wanted."

Her eyes shoot to mine. "Nash, I don't want to talk about my marriage or my late husband."

But he got you, and you had a baby with him.

"You two were always going to be something."

She begins to pace back and forth. "That makes it easier for you, doesn't it?"

That boil begins inside of me, and only she can cause it. "This isn't about me."

"It is. Because you know Zac and I always cared for one another—"

"He was madly in love with you," I state the truth, and it was my downfall too.

She laughs cynically to herself. "Maybe so, but he and I…"

"What? Just roommates who shared a bed?" Now I sound like a jealous son of a bitch.

Her jaw drops, as it should because my sentence came from the offside, even for me.

"You would think that, wouldn't you," she snarls.

"No point in arguing this. We have a wish to fulfill."

She shakes her head once, twice, with astonishment flooding her face. "You're really going to do it, aren't you? Move into the home Zac left me. You feel some sort of guilt and now here we are."

Now I'm fuming, and I step toward her, towering over her petite frame with her eyes sliding up to meet mine. She smells of mango, a peculiar smell, but that's always been her shampoo… always.

"It's not guilt."

Summer jabs her finger against my chest, her stare

carving into me. "It is. Because you're the one who let me go — You changed the path."

I'm quick to grab Summer's wrist, and her breath catches. I swear my chest is about to burst from the spike of my pulse, and I do at least 100 reps on the bench press on a daily basis to raise my heart rate. "Now isn't the time to rehash events," I warn her.

Crap. Are we having a confrontation for the whole world to see? The guests on the second floor must be getting a show.

A sly smirk begins to form on her beautiful mouth, and it concerns me but sucks me in all the same. "We'll have to eventually if you plan on living back in Lake Spark."

"But not today." Our eyes are in a tight latch again, and the air seems to evaporate around us. This is why I've stayed away. "Does it matter anyhow?"

"Nash, what have we been thrown into? What has your brother done?" Her voice grows delicate.

"Damage, without even knowing it," I rasp.

The joke's on us, it has to be.

"He always loved games." Everything softens inside of her. "Gosh, remember how he insisted on playing the old-school version of that video game where the kid is a paperboy for like a week?" she reflects and has a small wry smile.

My entire body eases. "Such a geek like that. He should have been dating, he had the looks. Instead, he could master every single card game and boardgame, too. I do remember that he nearly lost it when you informed him that there was a second version of the game. And remember how he had those ridiculous drawings?"

We both chuckle softly, and the air around us lightens.

But then her eyes abandon me to glance down to see my hand still wrapped around her wrist. I drop my fingers away like a burn to the skin then clear my throat, and we both step back to create some distance.

She clears her throat. "Fine." Her tone is curt.

"Fine what?"

"If you suddenly feel like you owe something to Zac, then move your bags on in and get to know your nephew." She doesn't sound thrilled, more deflated. "That's the *only* reason. To honor Zac's wishes because he loved Bo, and he wants you to know your nephew. For Zac and Bo," she clarifies.

My tongue darts to the corner of my mouth. I could scream that Zac owes me more. Alas, right now, it's about Summer who just received the bombshell she was never warned about.

"I'm moving in." That's my answer.

Against all better judgment.

"Honorable," she snipes as she shuffles her feet and walks a few paces with her back facing me as she looks at the water along the side of the dock.

I go from zero to a hundred around this woman. Tormented, angered, then hopelessly at her mercy; if only she knew. "It will be good for Bo, and you'll get a little relief."

A bitter noise rumbles from her throat. "Relief? You've got to be kidding me. You've stormed back into my life on a full-time basis."

Staring up at the sky, I then bow my head from exhaustion. "Like you were with my brother on a full-time basis?"

Her head darts in my direction, with her fumed expression cannonballing into me. "Listen." She clenches her fists in pure anger. "Let's be super clear from the get-go. We all were close at one time. You and me? We were supposed…" Summer can't muster the words, and I don't want her to.

The pain drips from every word. "But you were a coward. Your brother and I were friends. He did feel more, and I loved him differently. I wouldn't change the fact that our marriage…" She keeps doing that, as if she realizes what she is about to say but she doesn't want to. "Zac got to experience a marriage and fatherhood," she simply states.

Only because I let him have you.

I close my lids tightly, only to open them, wishing I could turn the clock back. "Don't say anything more."

"Fine." She's not impressed.

I can't even respond, which she takes as her cue to end this conversation. Summer pivots and grumbles as she leaves. "See you at *home*."

I can't help feeling that something isn't right. She's holding onto something she doesn't want me to know.

3

NASH

I lean against the reception desk inside the hotel. The man behind the desk whose name tag reads Stuart is busy swiping the tablet. I'm waiting patiently, but I crack a smile when Holden walks in my direction.

"Hey there, I heard you were back in town." He pats my shoulder and joins me at the desk.

"Where did you hear that?"

He scratches the back of his neck. "I have my sources."

I grin. "How bad is it?"

"Yeah, okay. I might have heard the other day when my wife and Summer were chatting about your mysterious impending arrival back at Lake Spark."

"Ah… and considering I just saw Summer, should I give it ten or twenty minutes before Lexi phones you with the latest news?"

Holden slants his head to the side and quirks his lips out. "Meh, it's school pick-up time, so probably twenty-five minutes."

Despite my absence in almost everything around this

town, I know Holden and Stone, the other investor, well enough.

Holden's face turns serious for a moment. "As much as I'm not impressed with your lack of involvement at the Dizzy Duck, that was always what you wished for, and we agreed on it from the start. That means we don't need to have any awkward business conversations. I can just ask, how are you holding up?"

"I'm doing okay. It's my brother's uncanny knack to turn his passing into a time of… well, I'm not sure, but he made mourning easy until now," I explain.

"Okay, that's you all checked out," Stuart, the receptionist, interrupts.

Holden's brows furrow. "You just got here. I kind of thought that you would at least check on the place that you have some stake in?"

I hand Stuart my key, as the Dizzy Duck stuck to classic keys instead of upgrading to keycards. I glance at Holden. "No, I will be around more for the next few weeks. I'll discover what I've missed and understand how you've made this place better than my parents ever would have."

He grins and pats my shoulder. "Now that's what I want to hear. We can have an informal meeting with Stone and catch up, plus go over some ideas for the coming months."

"Sounds like a plan, and it will keep me busy I guess." I shrug.

Holden's smile fades, and his face turns puzzled. "Wait, what? You're staying longer term? Why aren't you staying here?"

"I have a new place that I'll be lodging at."

"Where might that be?"

I can *almost* find humor in all of this. "Turns out my

brother's request is that I move in with Summer for a bit. Ensure she and Bo are doing okay."

Holden has no words as he looks at me with a blank face, his brows raised.

With my knuckles curled, I bump his arm. "It's okay. Say nothing. You're doing far better at taking the news than Summer did. And I'm too hyped up on adrenaline to even contemplate how this day is going."

"Cookie?" Stuart asks as he holds up a basket, oblivious to the tone of our conversation. I forgot he was in earshot.

"Not the time, Stuart." But they are great chocolate chip cookies that guests get at arrival and departure, even at turn-down service. I reach over. "You know what, give me a cookie." I slant a shoulder up. "For the road," I justify.

"Damn, that's a little crazy," Holden finally comments.

I take a bite of the sweet goodness. "I know, right? My brother conspires even from beyond. Kind of never thought he had it in him, but alright, on this ride I shall go. I'm sure Summer and I can keep enough distance between us. We'll just get into a routine, honor my brother, ignore our past, pretend all is well," I list with a full mouth, treating this moment far too casually because that's how I'm adjusting to shock.

"I don't even know the background of…" His eyes swim side to side. "Doesn't she kind of hate you?"

My lips roll into my mouth, and I tip my head to the side in contemplation. "Probably." Because there are no labels when it comes to my history with Summer, everyone just assumes we dislike one another.

Holden looks relieved with my answer. "Anything I can do?"

I shake my head. "Nah." I hold up my cookie. "Just save me when the shock wears off," I plead.

"You got it," he says as I brush past him.

But then I stall when I get a few steps further and pivot on the balls of my feet.

"Hey, Holden." I'm not sure I want to hear the answer of what I'm about to ask. He stares at me, waiting. "Summer… how has she been holding up?"

He scratches his chin. "Oh, I guess she's doing better than we would all expect. Keeps herself busy. Focuses on Bo. You know… she's been eager to move her life forward." His shoulder raises then drops. "I'm not sure if it's a cover or not, nor do I have any idea what it's like for her when she heads home. But here at the inn, she manages to smile."

Relief hits me. I'm not sure I could handle another answer. I've always stayed away to save us all, and if I were to blow back into town needing to rescue Summer, then I'm not sure I would have it in me to keep things on a neutral level with her.

"Thanks. Well… I, uh… I should go."

His eyes seem to study me, and he nods once. If it's understanding that he is offering, then I'll take it.

KNOCKING ON THE DOOR, I'm still wondering why I'm standing here about to embark on a request from my brother.

The door opens, and Summer's scowl greets me, but for a few ticks our eyes hold in silence.

"I'm here. Can I come in?"

She steps to the side and holds the door open. "Surprised you asked since this is now your home, too." Zero enthusiasm seeped through those words.

I mosey past her, and already I'm observing the setting as we walk into the living area. Examining the room, it's cozy and airy. The wood of the shelves is painted white, and the floors are a light pine shade. A contrast to the dark pines surrounding the house as seen through the double doors in the living room.

"And here we are. Nash knocking on our door and waltzing on in to uproot our lives."

"That's what you think. I'll always be the villain in your book." I give her a steely stare.

Rage brews inside of her, and I see her face etched in annoyance. "It's because this request is near insanity. When I got married, you sent a damn waffle maker with a note."

"It's a classic wedding gift," I defend coolly.

She's not amused. "When Bo was born, you sent a stuffed proboscis monkey and a note. Who the hell sends the ugliest freakiest choice when a normal monkey should have sufficed."

I shrug, and I'm doing my best to shove down a smirk. "It's different."

"And now you want to upgrade to moving in? I'm surprised you didn't just drop a note with one sentence through the mailbox to inform me. It's more your style," she says dryly.

Feisty Summer. It doesn't happen often, except when she's around me.

I don't answer, instead pinching the bridge of my nose and bowing my head down.

"Now if you'll excuse me, Bo is waking up."

By the time I lift my eyes, she's already whizzed away.

Slowly I walk around the living room, and my eyes pause when I see the basket of baby toys in the corner. I've seen Bo once now, at my brother's funeral. What a shitty uncle I've been. I know that I need to rectify that.

The patter of steps down the stairs draws my gaze up to

see Summer walking into the room holding Bo who looks wide awake, holding the monkey.

"Oh, look at that, someone enjoys his freaky monkey." I smile confidently and raise my brows at Summer.

She rolls her eyes and bounces him on her hip, choosing to ignore me. "This is your uncle." She sighs. "He's moving in." Her tone is impassive, and she picks up his little hand to wave. "I know, what a surprise." Tone still unchanged.

I step forward to touch my nephew gently, and the corner of my mouth hitches up. Bo makes a sound that is promising for me.

"Hey, buddy, you probably don't remember me, but I'm your uncle." I grab his loose shirt delicately. He's wiggly in Summer's arms, so he acts as a barrier between her and me.

But still, my eyes flick up and catch Summer soaking in the scene, as if she's been waiting for this. Maybe so, I'm blood-related to this little guy who is smiling at me, and that lightens the feeling in my chest too.

Summer clears her throat. "Uhm… he probably needs a snack, so we should go do that."

I step back. "Of course."

A few minutes later, my nephew is staring at me with marvel in his eyes. He smiles a lot, especially when he's sitting in his highchair squishing banana between his fingers. Bo is going to be the spitting image of my brother, I can tell.

"So, buddy, looks like you and I are going to be hanging out more." I hold my clenched fist up. "No? No fist bump?" I joke as I sit next to him at the kitchen table.

"You two will get along well. He doesn't respond with words, so you'll be in your element, spewing out sentences with nobody to debate you." Summer brings the rim of her tea mug to her lips, but I can see the smug grin that she's trying to hide.

"Cute." A contrite smile is pasted on my mouth. She's angry at me for staying away for so long, and I don't blame her.

"Uhm, so…" Awkwardness begins. "I'm going to head back to Chicago for a day or two to gather some things and wrap up some meetings with my agent."

Lines form on her forehead. "I thought your hockey days are over."

"They are, but I still have a few sponsor commitments."

Her head tips slightly to the side. "Right."

"Just let me know which room I'm moving into."

An amused look greets me. "Subtle."

Shaking my head, I'm now completely drained by her attitude. "I'm not trying to figure out which room you decided to make a baby in, if that's what you are wondering."

Shit. That came out cruel and envious.

Her mouth gapes open, yet she contains her composure. "Unbelievable. You really are a piece of work."

"Not sure I'm the only one."

Summer's cheeks puff out. "I don't have time for this. I have laundry to do and a bottle of white to drown in when Bo goes to sleep tonight. But for your information, you can take the guest room across from Bo's room. It's never been used."

I'm not sure if that brings ease or is more oil thrown on the fire as I puzzle together the history of sleeping arrangements in this house, even though Summer has only been living here since around the time my brother passed. But it's the mere thought of them that…

Summer marches to Bo, ignoring the fact that she's pushing me out of the way, practically on top of me as I sit, and she reaches to unbuckle Bo from his highchair. Her body stretching too close to me drives my body haywire in epic proportions.

"Come on, cutie. Let's go play in the living room." She throws a glare over her shoulder. "My son is the cutie, in case you need every detail to be explained."

"Spirited as always." My tone is flat.

She props Bo against her hip before she grumbles and walks away.

I rub my face with my hands. I have to get a grip. We won't be able to live together like this.

I've always watched Summer from afar to lessen the sting. But now she's way too close for my resolve.

I heave a sigh and slide off the chair, knowing I'm going to have to face her one more time today for good measure. Plus, I need to walk through the living room to get to the front door.

Walking into the living room, I stop in my tracks when I see Summer sitting on the floor, her hair down and feathering her arms. She's making noises at Bo, and they're both giggling while she wiggles his captured foot. She was always meant to be a mom. She's a natural, and this is an image of two happy souls. Despite what's happened, they deserve this moment.

Even if Summer doesn't want to admit it, she's hurting from my brother's passing too. And Bo? Well, he'll never remember his father. My heart aches for too many reasons, but I won't let Summer be the reason this time. I owe it to my brother to be the man who watches over his family.

My eyes slide to the side, and something captures my eye. Taking a few steps, I pause when I notice a photo of Summer, Zac, and Bo, the three of them together when Bo must have been a few weeks old. They're a family in the photo with affection on their faces. But the photo next to them, it's clear. No need to see it up close.

The three of *us*. My brother, Summer, and me.
Long ago.
When this mess all began.
And it all comes back…

(4)

NASH

Don't torture yourself. You knew they would be here, and still you decide to join when you saw them. Damn it, Nash.

I slow my walk as I approach Summer and Zac sitting on the edge of the dock. My brother's legs dangling and Summer sitting cross-legged half turned to face him. They are deep in conversation, but Summer's eyes slide in my direction, then she does a double take. Her eyes are laced with fear and delight that I'm here.

My brother shoots his gaze up and an instant beaming smile forms.

"Oh hey, I thought you would be at the rink." My brother scoots over to make room for me to join, and I sit on his other side cross-legged to face Summer as my brother leans back on his elbows.

"Finished early. It's the off season. I was just focusing on practicing skills and concentration. Can't work too hard," I explain. It's been five years since I went pro, but it still feels good to come home in the summer.

My brother shrugs it off. "I was just telling Summer about a BBQ I want to throw later. Remember in high school, when our parents would be complete idiots and leave us alone on the weekends? They kept giving us prime opportunities for parties and stuff," he reflects.

Zac is right, someone should have given them the parenting-a-teenager playbook.

One person's stupidity is another person's gain, right? It meant at the end of my senior year, it gave me ample opportunity for a stolen moment with Summer that stayed in my mind, but we left it in the past.

Until a few months ago.

"Anyway, I think we'll all go easy tonight with a few friends and throw some burgers on the grill. Nothing like the way you normally celebrate a game win," my brother explains.

Last season I only celebrated with Summer because we happened one night. My little brother's best friend who has always occupied my thoughts. It was a kiss in the making, a pop of the tension bubble between us, and it quickly turned to more. We kissed once when we were younger, but this was zero to a hundred within a minute.

It should have only been a hook-up, but I've been addicted to Summer ever since.

We've just kept it quiet, as we weren't sure how Zac would react. Maybe it was our logic that we would only be a fling and he would never need to know.

But it's no longer what we imagined.

Summer clears her throat. "I'm sure people just want to hang out. No need to break out the shots."

"I'm sure that's how Nash rolls between games. Girls are

always all over him. They must buy him shots." My brother's words agitate Summer, and I can tell because of the way she nibbles her bottom lip to hide her disdain at the thought.

"How were your classes this morning?" I divert the conversation and stare down at the wood. My brother is taking extra classes because he's in medical school and is about to start clinical rotations.

Summer laughs. "You're too smart for me," she teases Zac.

Zac looks between us, then his eyes land on Summer. "You guys won't be laughing when I'm a doctor and you both need me to save you."

"Whoa, I'm never trusting you, even if you have a stethoscope around your neck," she pushes back in good humor, and it makes him grin more.

My eyes catch Summer's, and my brother is oblivious. It's been happening a lot the past few weeks. We get to have a few seconds of connection before one of has to tear our sight away, and this time it's me when Zac pushes off the dock.

"I have to head in. Need like an hour more of study time. I'll hit the store on my way home."

When Zac stands and looks down, he takes a moment to look between us. His expression is peculiar; I don't recognize it, but when he smiles softly again, then ease hits me.

"See ya." I tip my nose up.

"Later, Zac."

He gives Summer an extra smile. "Don't look too hot tonight, otherwise Nash and I will be too busy playing bodyguard."

Her face blossoms red, but she plays it cool. "I'll do my best to suppress my superpowers." She salutes him.

By the time he's out of sight, my full attention is on

Summer who will not be having anyone's fingers but my own touching her tonight.

I admire the way Summer's lips twist when she blushes, and the way her eyes attempt to escape my watch is one of the most beautiful things I've seen. Her head tips to the side as she examines me, waiting for me to say something.

I place the palm of my hand on her thigh below the hem of her jean shorts, not caring that we're on the dock at the Dizzy Duck Inn on a warm summer's day. I lean in to steal a kiss. I need her lips on mine. The way I've needed her every time we manage to see one another. During the end of the season, she would tell Zac she was visiting a friend from college, but really, she was with me when my game schedule would allow.

She always melts under the command of my mouth, always following my cues, as if I will lead the way and be her protector. Her trust in me runs strong.

No matter how hard I kiss her, her lips always remain soft and silky. Even when I'm inside of her going hard, she still captures my mouth so delicately.

Right now, she scoots closer to me, causing our knees to touch to ensure that we are inseparable.

One more second. That's all I get before we need air. Pulling apart, my hand stays put on the back of her neck, with my thumb caressing her cheek.

"Nash," she tuts. "Anyone can see."

"And? My parents own this place. We've also agreed that Zac should probably know, we just need to find the right moment."

She nods her head in complete agreement. "*Finally*. I've begged you for weeks to tell him."

My jaw flexes at the uncomfortable reminder. "It's just…

you two have been friends forever. He thinks I look at you like a little sister."

Summer's eyes widen. "Well, I'm sure he will change his view when he discovers you fucked me in the family pool house the other week, and then we agreed that our theory is true and that we're quite good at it together. Hence, why we fuck like crazy."

Summer, my spitfire Summer. I need to thank someone upstairs.

I chuckle and glance up at the sky then back to Summer who is smirking. "You have such a mouth."

She gives me a funny look. "Like you're one to talk." Her smile stays fixed as her eyes squinch from the sun, the breeze off the lake blowing her hair behind her shoulders. "You're leaving soon," she reminds me. Hockey season is not a friend to any relationship.

"We'll make it work." I shrug.

Her blue eyes sparkle at my insistence, and she interlaces our fingers, with her eyes set on our hands as if she is taking a mental picture, but she doesn't answer.

I guide her to turn toward me. "Let's not discuss it any more today. When I'm away, I'll still be possessive of you. You're like a hockey puck I won't let anyone touch."

Her head falls back when she cracks a laugh. "Oh my gosh, you did not just compare your gorgeous fuck to a puck."

"Summer, language," I chide to tease her. We begin to walk back toward the shore, and I nudge her shoulder with mine. "Come on, we have a window of a few hours."

And we take advantage of it. A few hours later, I'm looking in the mirror as I run my fingers through my hair. It's apparent by my flushed look that I've just had sex, and a small smirk of pride hits the corner of my mouth as I slide back into my boxer briefs.

It's a little crazy that I'm back in my family home, but my parents are gone to their house in North Carolina. I have plenty of money to get my own place for the summer, but I just want downtime and the familiar, away from city life. And this room has memories. A first kiss with Summer, and now a few years later, I step back into the room to see her sitting up in bed with her feet on the floor as she attempts to clasp her bra closed.

I dive on top of the bed on my side and take over to help her, then I gently kiss the curve of her shoulder.

An unusual silence fills the room until she breaks it. "Nash, I feel something strong. I know that I'm in—"

I cut her off instantly and plant my finger on her mouth, not wanting to hear the words. "I feel it, too."

She twists her body to glance down to me. "You have me. Every part, and don't you dare break it." Her lips skim my bottom lip.

She means her heart.

5

SUMMER

I adjust the few flowers that I just set on the grave.

"I know, I know. I'm being a complete, well…" I ponder to myself and even roll my eyes. "A bitch, if I'm being really honest. But your brother is returning it in full."

Speaking to Zac's grave seems to be a weekly occurrence for me. But it's never tears, no. Oh no, he would never have that.

"Every time, I want to lay it on the table. And I know I should, but… I'm scared of his reaction."

The truth is too easy.

"It's the same as you, I guess. You never told me you loved me until you were sick. Before then you chickened out, and I didn't feel I needed to press. Anyhow, Bo will be excited to have Nash here. He also thinks O-shaped cereal is the greatest thing on earth, so perhaps his standards are low. You know, Bo still loves to look at the photo on the mantle of you, Nash, and me. We were so young and naïve then, weren't we? Oh, and did I tell you that we had a guest at the Dizzy Duck who screamed to her husband that she wanted a divorce? We all know, because it happened in the restaurant… where the husband and his mistress were having dinner. These are the kinds of things that keep me moving."

My eyes draw a line up to the sky, admiring the clear blue, then I return to the gray stone. "I wonder if you're mad at me up there for never telling you about me and Nash before you died. You probably get all of the best secrets up there, don't you? I have a feeling I should brace myself. What are you up to?"

I trace my fingers over the lettering on the stone. "Until next time." I smile to myself.

Leaving the graveyard, I take a deep breath. It's odd, but I always feel calm after visiting. It's quiet here. I don't follow any religion, but if there is something in our afterlife, then I would like to think everyone here has found solace.

Deciding to take the long walk, I wander along the lake and then up Main Street. A freshly brewed coffee is in order, and when I walk through the door of Jolly Joe's, with the bell dinging, I inhale the smell of the place as my eyes take in the 50s-style diner and hope someone picked a good song on the jukebox.

It's still early enough in the day, which means the smell of coffee and cinnamon rolls runs strong. It's so silly, but they place little jellybeans in every single cup of coffee because apparently it brings luck.

"The usual?" Mary, behind the counter, asks. She's worked here for as long as I can remember.

"Yes, please. No cinnamon roll today." I smile.

"Sure thing, kiddo. By the way," she begins as she holds up a mug, and I know where this is going. Now is the time to plaster on a fake smile. "I heard Nash was back in town."

Yep, there it is.

"He is." My smile is strained.

"Hmm." That's how she manages to respond? I would say I got off easy, but she seems to be examining me and forming an internal theory.

Ignoring her, I slide into a booth and remove my scarf. I texted Lexi on my way here to see if she was in town, but I didn't hear back.

I have to smile to myself as I sit here. It's nostalgic, and you always know what you'll get. I thank Mary when she places the coffee in front of me and look up in pleasant surprise when I see Harlow, another friend, stepping through the door.

"Hey there, can I join you?"

"Please." I sound relieved because it means I won't have to listen to Mary share her observations.

Harlow smiles politely at Mary in passing before joining me at the table. Harlow is married to Stone who owns part of the Dizzy Duck, and she's also an author.

"I've been craving an orange roll since two am this morning," she groans.

My face forms lines. "Two am?"

She tucks her light brown locks behind her ear then looks down at her belly. "This thing won't let me sleep."

I chuckle at her. "Thing. You mean baby?"

"Baby, thing, does it matter? I can't sleep, and I still have another two months to go."

"It's a special time." I raise a shoulder.

She waves me off and captures Mary's attention then points to the orange rolls on display.

"So, how are you? I heard a special guest checked into the Dizzy Duck, only to check back out." She flashes me a look.

That's what I appreciate about my friends. They don't treat me like I'm fragile. I've made it clear that I want to have normalcy in my life, and they follow my lead; hence, why she can tease me about a fact that shouldn't be funny at all. Yet, if I were in her shoes, I would do the same.

"I'm surprised the mayor hasn't put up a billboard yet to welcome Nash back. But yes, he rolled into town and now apparently gets a key to my house, too." I take a long sip of my coffee.

Harlow's eyes bug out. "Why?"

"It's Zac's wish to have his brother move in for six weeks."

"Huh, he didn't talk about this at all before he passed?"

I shake my head. "No. Don't think he would have, actually. From what I gather, it's a sort of brotherly tribal thing, you know, step in when the other cannot. I'm just surprised that Zac would think I need a protector."

She taps her flawless manicured olive-green nails on the table. "I mean, you all used to be friends, right?"

I huff a sound. "Something like that…"

A friendship too far, perhaps.

So many things where I should have put my foot down, but I didn't, especially three years ago, and recalling it still brings mixed emotions.

I nearly tumble onto the chair at Catch 22, the restaurant on the lake that's half casual and half sophisticated. I'm late.

"So, so, soooo sorry." I'm panting after hurrying from my car to here where Zac is waiting. "There was a family of ducks crossing the road, and you know how I get. Have to stop for ducks. I mean, who doesn't in Lake Spark? Did you hear that there is a coyote that's been rampaging through people's garbage at night?"

He smiles wryly as I ramble, and he waits patiently for me to stop. When I set my purse on the empty chair at the table, he takes it as his cue to speak. "You are a noble citizen. And we all had the extra section on our drivers test in regard to stopping for Lake Spark wildlife."

I smile brightly. "See?" I grab the glass of water and take a quick sip. "I'm happy you picked this place for our weekly brunch. I want to try the new chicken salad."

That's us. We see one another on a regular basis. One another's ride-or-die.

"I'm going to head right into it. I have to ask you something."

His sentence grabs my attention. "Shoot. What's up?"

Zac swipes his fingers across his jaw as he hesitates. "You and Nash."

I nearly spit out the ice cube in my mouth as my body freezes. His name gives me this reaction every single time, yet I attempt to be unaffected.

"What about him?" The room feels cold. "If this is about Nash living in his own world, then just, you know, let it go, or you can reach out. I'm sure you both will renew your brotherly bond."

The thorn in my side. Nash breaking my heart then distancing himself from Lake Spark altogether. I know he has an investment in the Dizzy Duck, it was their parents' stipulation when they sold the place.

"It's not that. Although, I wish we were at a better place. He has his hockey career." A pit in my stomach always forms when we talk about him. "Nothing ever happened between you and him, right?"

My heart sinks. A lie is a lie, but for some reason, Nash and I decided long ago that it's better for Zac. Not even sure why I went along with it, but I keep my feet firmly planted for stability against the lie that is about to spew from my mouth. "No, of course not."

Relief fills his eyes. "Sorry. Of course." A half-smile

breaks out. "I mean, at the random family functions when he graces us with his presence, you two look like you might kill each other. And to be honest, I wouldn't like it if you two had some history. In fact, I would hate it. I'm too protective of you, and my brother isn't always great news when it comes to the female population."

Oh, I know. Preaching to the choir.

"I know you've clarified this many times, it's just lately..." He rolls his shoulder back then subtly shakes his head. "I'm being crazy."

That's why we haven't told him. No need to crush him. I'm not blind, I know Zac loves me in a different way, he's just never openly admitted it, and still, it hasn't affected our friendship.

Swallowing, I remind myself to bury Nash deeper inside of me, as he surfaces too much in my thoughts when someone brings him up. "Anyhow, was that all, detective?" I manage to bring back my bright and cheery voice.

Zac seems to chuckle under his breath, and his eyes circle the room as he seems to be finding words. "You know I would do anything for you, right?"

"Of course. And I return the sentiment in full." I beam.

"Then I have the world's most extreme favor to ask." His face shades to pleading.

My eyes narrow as I try to figure out where this conversation is going. "Okay, and..." It draws out.

"It's more that I need a favor to ensure that everything is set for a life insurance policy should..."

"Did the doctor say something?" My heart sinks for the second time in this conversation, but this time it's all devoted to Zac. Fear fills me at record speed. He's been healthy for years, but it doesn't surprise me that there could always be a recurrence or it leading to something else.

He doesn't need to say any words, his face says it all. "The thing is, I have this long list of things that I wanted in life but…"

I stare at him blankly. "What's on the list?"

"You… Marry me."

———

HARLOW WAVES a hand in front of my face. "Uhm, are you okay?"

My eyes flicker. "Oh yeah, totally."

Not really. Did I do the right thing? I married my best friend. I couldn't say no because of an overbearing feeling of caring for him while he was ill. I was naïve to think that he was supposed to get better. I wasn't supposed to feel that I wanted a child and that he would be a great father. Zac was optimistic he would be okay, until he told me when I was very pregnant that he didn't have long left.

Harlow sinks into the booth. "You know if you need a break or something, just send Bo our way. I'd be happy to take care of him if you need rest or…"

I look at her, unimpressed but still with a humored smile. "I'm sure you mean if Nash and I need to have a serious discussion?"

"No," she lies, her voice uneven, then she takes a second before she gives in. "Totally," she says bluntly.

That causes the corners of my mouth to tug up. Twirling some hair around my finger, I do my best to sink into my current life status. "I should have thought about this more. I mean, not just agreeing that he could move in."

"Maybe. But if it's in his will, can you even do anything? How do those things work?"

A short laugh escapes me. "I'm still processing the

request a little more. Instead, my mouth didn't connect with my brain, and I found myself agreeing to it."

She shrugs. "Maybe that's a good thing. Our brains are the last to catch up. Besides, wouldn't you want Bo to be around his family?"

I hold my mug up to her. "Exactly that." Harlow waits for me to continue because she can tell that I'm about to rant, and I do. "We will just have to set some rules, go over schedules, and he will need to learn that we work around Bo's needs. And he has to work on his baby-caring skills. Do you think I can leave him alone with Bo yet?" I bring a finger to my chin, also recognizing that they had an instant connection. "Of course not, silly thought. He probably doesn't even know how to change a diaper. Oh, and he absolutely better not leave dirty dishes in the sink."

Harlow taps her nails on the table. "You might need to slow down. I think you first need to make him a spare key," she points out.

"Ugh, this is not happening." I collapse onto the table with an innate need to bang my head for show.

Harlow gently pets my head. "Unexpected things can bring sadness, but they can also bring the best things in life," she mentions softly.

I raise my head to look at her.

Because what she says is crazy, ridiculous… and probably true.

COULDN'T HE USE A DOORBELL? But *noooo,* let's just knock.

It stirs up some therapeutic nonsense that someone offered after Zac's passing. I vaguely remember the words that knocks means right decisions, positive change, a message from a spirit, a soul mate…

Huffing out a breath, I open the door with gusto.

"It's me… again." Nash has an uncomfortable look on his face.

I crane my neck and tip my nose up to search for his luggage. "Changed your mind? There are no suitcases."

Nash steps through the threshold without a care in the world. "In my car, and I'll get it later."

Closing the door, I follow him to the living room where he plops himself onto the couch as if he owns the place.

"Where's Bo?"

"Sleeping. He does that a lot in case you're wondering. Speaking of which, what is your experience with babies on a scale of one to ten?"

"Probably a two." He doesn't seem bothered. At least he's honest.

"And how do you want to handle the schedule? Are you just going to come and go as you please?"

He kicks his feet up on the coffee table, bringing his crossed arms behind his head, and I stomp right over and strip his feet off back onto the floor. "I'll work around you guys, handle everything I need to while I'm in Lake Spark."

"Fine." I pick up a baby blanket on the floor and begin to fold it to keep my hands occupied. "Dishwasher and garbage, those are your chores."

Nash chuckles. "Didn't realize I would have a sticker chore chart. Do I get ice cream at the end of the week if I'm good?" He's mocking me.

I throw him a tight smile. "Funny."

He leans forward and rests his elbows on his knees, his hands hanging between his thighs. "Seriously, do you need anything? The house all good?"

I take myself down a notch to bring neutrality to the room. "It's fine. I've only had this house since right before Zac passed. He was insistent that he buy it, and in a rush, too. We didn't have a lot of time once he found out that he was terminal. In fact, in the end, he didn't even sleep here since I moved in while he was in the hospital. Still, I'm sure his spirit is here."

Nash seems to register my meaning. "He wanted to ensure you and Bo were taken care of."

I toss the blanket onto the arm of the sofa, giving up on folding it properly. "That's him. He kept saying to me *'Don't worry, Summer. I've made sure that you have everything you'll need, I promise.'*" The pure thought causes my lips to curve.

Perching on the sofa arm almost exhausted, I reach up to find the charm of my necklace to twist between my fingers.

"Everything made sense in his head," Nash notes.

"So it seems." I bring my charm to my mouth, a habit.

"What is it?"

At first, I don't understand, but then I see Nash with his eyes set on my fingers.

"This?" I hold it up and affection warms my face. "It's a treasure chest." Nash seems surprised, and his eyes widen slightly. "Zac got it for me."

To me it's normal, but Nash's eyes are lasered in on my chain, and most of all, I can't help but notice his eyes have darkened. A shiver runs down my body all the way to my toes.

"A lucky guess on the charm since I never mentioned my ridiculous theory of the mystical lake. He got it for me after we…"

I don't finish the sentence because I can already see that Nash is lost in thoughts, or worse, memories.

NASH

"We're going to miss your presence during hockey season. We're still holding out that you'll get traded to the Spinners here in town." One of the guys from the ice rink holds his cup up amongst the chatter. The kitchen is buzzing with a few of Zac's friends as we talk around the kitchen island with drinks and chips with dip.

"We should have just made this a goodbye party to our town's royalty." My brother sounds almost annoyed.

Summer nudges Zac from where she's leaning against the countertop next to him. "Don't be a grumpy old man."

My brother's eyes flare up at her, unimpressed by her comment.

I step forward and pat my brother's shoulder. "Come on, little brother, let's go check if the BBQ is ready to grill the burgers."

Zac sighs. "Sure. I could use some fresh air."

Summer gives me a nervous nod but stays put, and my

heart heats in anticipation of this conversation, and the endgame is that I can kiss her in the open right after it's all done.

My brother needs to know.

When we're outside, the music from inside simmers down, and despite two or three friends perched on the steps on the other side of the pool, it's quiet enough.

My brotherly senses ring an alarm bell because Zac just doesn't seem himself, or at least not the same guy as earlier today.

I squeeze his shoulder and guide him to sit down on a chair. "Everything okay? You seem a little off tonight."

He shakes his shoulders and adjusts his neck as if he can rid the tension. "It's fine. It's just…" He's agitated for sure. "It's Summer."

My brows rise. "What about her?" Does he already know?

Zac sighs. "Tonight's the night, tonight's the night that the truth has to come out."

"Look, Zac, about Summer and—"

"I'm going to make my move," he interjects.

My entire body jolts from surprise. "W-what do you mean?" There is an edge in my voice of concern and fear.

"You've seen the way I look at her. I know you have. You keep examining us with your eyes. You've got to see it, that she and I could be more."

Nausea hits my stomach. "I… don't know."

He leans back into the chair, sulking. "Of course, you wouldn't know. At the snap of your fingers, you have it all. I don't think she and I were meant to be friends. Our connection is too strong and only gets stronger as the years go by."

I swipe my hand across my jaw, now stuck behind a difficult rock. "What if she doesn't want that?"

My brother seems to contemplate, and even he doesn't know. "It's… she's been different lately. I feel like it's a sign that I can be honest with her. Do you think she's seeing someone?" Swallowing, words get stuck in my throat, and I can't answer. "I think I might kill the guy that gets to kiss her."

"I never knew you felt this way about her."

"She never gave an indication that maybe she would be interested, so I kept it all in. But, for sure, she's been so happy lately, and it has to be…"

I clench my fist, doing my best to come up with a game plan for this turn of events. "What if I said I kissed her?" What the fuck just spun off my tongue?

Zac frowns yet doesn't seem concerned. "You wouldn't do that to me. Nah, you're just throwing hypotheticals at me. Besides, you're leaving for your hockey career, and that would just leave Summer here all alone. Not to mention, you would never let a girl come between us." He eases as if my sentence was crazy, but his facts are correct too, and a hint of doubt begins to hit me. "High school sucked, I was home a lot sick. Then college and medical school are stressful as hell, but maybe now I get to have something great in my life. For once, I can be the guy who is luckier than you."

My stomach fills with nausea. If I admit the truth now, then he will be shattered. And he's already had a few bad years. What have I done? I had no clue he was interested, except deep down, I probably did but kept it locked up.

"I mean, with you busy with your hockey career, we don't see one another as much. But Summer? We seem to bond closer," he continues, but my ears seem to be buzzing.

I'm his big brother. I've watched him suffer, and I feel guilty that it wasn't me. He seems excited and happy. Even though I know Summer isn't interested, they will be together more than I will with Summer, that's what my professional life does. I don't want him to be alone. Because even if he makes a move, Summer will laugh it off and get them back on track as friends.

Except if she's with me? He'll resent us both, and he'll be miserable.

Everything inside of me twists.

There is a long silence between us. My brother stares at me, and maybe he is reading my mind or he's completely oblivious, but it feels as though an unspoken warning seems to be sent from him.

And that's enough for me.

MY LIPS PART from the bruising kiss between me and Summer as we sit in the front of my car. Our noses nuzzle, and I wish I could take more.

"Don't do this," she whispers.

"You shouldn't have followed me." I'm desperate to get as far from her as possible. I barely drank, a few sips really. Getting away from the party and the house is the only way I might breathe tonight.

I shake my head, bracing myself for the struggle not to touch her as I sink back into my seat. "We can't make this work."

Summer sighs. "That's a lie. You're telling me that you spoke to Zac and now you say that we have no future. What aren't you telling me?" She's begged me to explain, but all I can do is break up with her and use a lie.

"I've thought about it more, with my hockey schedule and you living in Lake Spark. Zac just pointed out the obvious. There is no realistic way for us to work. You'll be miserable and so will I." I do my best to avoid her eyes.

She turns, with her sight landing on me as her head stays put against the headrest. I always love the way the light from my dashboard reflects off her beautiful face.

She turns away from me to look out the window, doing her best to stay composed.

"You can blame me, Summer," I rasp. I can't tear my eyes away from her as I watch her crumble. "I'm doing this so in the long run your heart doesn't break even harder."

An unamused sound leaves her lips. "So just do it now, is that it?"

I start the engine with every intention of taking her home. We need to part ways because the air around us is insufferable right now.

Unbearable silence fills my car as I drive us away from my house.

"You'll change your mind in the morning when you realize how much of a mistake this is," she tells me softly.

"I know you. You have a kind heart. Nor do you want to be that girl that gets between two brothers. Tell me that isn't true?" I challenge.

Her face bows down, and she goes quiet for a second. "You're right."

"It's why you will let me walk. You have to let me walk away."

"You'll change your mind."

My heart is ripping into pieces. "I won't, Summer." I feel my throat strain, as I don't want to talk but I have to. I swallow. "Sometimes we have to let go, and that's what we need to do. We had a few great months, but we need to just…"

The sound of her sniffling is torment. My entire body tenses, and I want to escape the vehicle.

But I can't because I feel the wheel of the car shift, and my hands lose grip as we swivel.

It happens so fast. And it isn't until we crash and the airbags deflate that I realize I must have lost grip of the wheel. I can't process if it's a tree we hit or something else, I'm not sure, because there are a thousand thoughts in my head.

I don't even worry about myself, even though I feel an ache somewhere. But when I glance to my side, my heart drops when I see Summer has blood gushing down her face.

———

I watch from the doorway of the hospital room with my arms crossed, leaning against the doorframe as the nurse finishes bandaging Summer's head. An airbag and a broken window caused Summer to need stiches that the doctor said will probably scar. There's bruising on her body, plus abrasions on her chin. Not to mention, her arm is probably going to ache for days. Are we lucky on the car crash front? We aren't on any other front.

Or at least me. Because of guilt.

Someone bumps into my shoulder, ignoring me, and it doesn't take long for me to see it's Zac. He storms straight to Summer and pauses for a moment as he looks at the nurse who gives him a smile as she gathers her things and gives them space.

Zac sweeps Summer's hand between his two palms. "Fuck, I was so worried. When Nash called, I nearly went out of my mind."

Summer groans as she attempts to sit further up, and my brother is quick to touch her arms to encourage her to slow down. "Sorry if we ruined your BBQ, hope you saved us some leftovers," she attempts to joke, but her voice is groggy.

"Not funny. I guess Nash was taking you home. Thankfully, he was there to help you." Zac glances back to me, and I can see the concern in his face. "It's miraculous that she's not in more pieces. We're lucky that you're okay and we can focus on Summer getting better."

Over his shoulder, I see Summer gawking her eyes at me. She wants me to say something, but I can't. It's my fault she's lying here. I broke her heart, and the anger within me caused me to lose focus on the road. All because I don't act normal around this woman.

"Relax, Zac, Mr. Future Doctor. I'll be fine. They want me to stay overnight for observation, but tomorrow I'll be good as new," Summer attempts to calm him.

My brother's eyes whip to Summer. "Not so easy. I want to check your vitals."

"You're a soon-to-be doctor if things go well. I think she's fine," I remind him. Partly, because I don't want him to study all the ways that Summer is in pain right now… because of my doing.

"I'm going to ignore him." Zac perches on the edge of the bed and holds Summer's hand tighter. "Summer, I would hate life if you weren't in it. You're everything to me."

She can't look at him. And my focus on Summer is boiling emotions inside of me. All I do is cause her pain. This has to be a sign, another reason that I made the right decision.

Zac is about to melt down because he cares more for this woman than anything. He loves and pines for her, that I'm sure of.

The thought already spins in my mind.

"We should probably let Summer sleep," I suggest softly.

"I'm not leaving her. They must be checking for a concussion."

A sound escapes Summer as she attempts to shift again. "Really, it will be fine. Nash was my superhero."

My brother circles his thumb on top of Summer's hand. "Doesn't matter. You're precious goods to me. Probably Nash, too… well, when he doesn't disappear for long periods of time for the hockey season. But you get my drift," he attempts to make a joke.

However, he's right again.

Summer's eyes soften to me, pleading, and maybe she already grasps my thoughts.

I'm no good for her. She deserves better. Around me, her life gets turned upside down.

Water begins to swell in the bottom of her eyes.

"Nash," she warns and pleads, her voice uneven and quiet.

Our eyes hold, and it hurts, but sometimes you have to close a door.

Maybe she's lucky.

Her scar that will be visible on her head will be nothing compared to the deep scar that I'll carry on my heart.

7

NASH

I can't tear my eyes away from the charm trapped between the pads of Summer's fingers. She just explained how she ended up with the necklace as if it's no big deal. Of course, she has no clue.

"I don't wear it every day, but still, it's special. I keep thinking maybe I should add my wedding ring to it." She splays her hand out in front of her to examine her fingers. I notice her fingers are bare; it causes me to wonder, but it makes it easier for me to return my attention to the necklace.

My throat bobs as I try to suppress the memory because I've had enough memories today. "It's pretty."

Summer gives me a peculiar look. "Uh, thanks." The air turns stiff, and she must feel it too because she stands up. "I'm going to grab a water, want anything?" Wow, she's being hospitable to me.

Gently, I shake my head as she patters past me, and unfortunately, my mind drifts to why she has the necklace.

"I want to get her something really nice. She's special, and after getting married, a ring just doesn't seem enough," my brother explains as we peruse the jewelry store.

I'm not sure why I'm doing this to myself. They eloped out of the blue, and I do my best to see them less and less. I've barely spoken to my brother, but Zac is in Dallas for a medical conference, and since I have a game here, we managed to squeeze in a quick lunch. And now I'm being dragged to a jewelry store.

"How is she?" I pry, with a sting inside of me.

Zac doesn't bother glancing up as he studies the contents of the glass case. "Good. She's been my rock and seems content with work and living in Lake Spark still."

I'm happy for her... and him. This is what was supposed to happen when I locked my heart from Summer. I still feel like I probably left pieces in my trail, even if for the long run it's the best for everyone. Doesn't mean she doesn't cross my mind more than she should.

"There it is." My brother taps on the glass with his long finger. "A charm necklace. Perfect for someone you love."

"Because she loves you too." I'm not sure why I need the clarification so quick.

He stalls and draws his gaze to me. "Of course." Why didn't that feel more confident? It's a long moment before he occupies himself with the contents under the glass. "I bet she would love the flower."

Peeking over his shoulder, I examine the choices, and then my eyes lock onto one particular choice.

"Can I have a look at the flower charm?" my brother requests to the lady who scurries our way.

"Of course." She unlocks the back of the display with a key that was around her neck on a lanyard. "Everyone loves these. At Christmas, we have presents and trees."

Pretending to look at my watch, I pat his shoulder. "I'm going to head out. Need to get ready for the game." And I don't want to watch you buy Summer jewelry, because you're in love with the woman who should have been mine.

He gives me a healthy smile while the jeweler sets the tray in front of him. "Sure thing. It was great seeing you. You have to come back to Lake Spark more often. We all miss you."

"Maybe."

I turn to walk away and manage a few steps when I hear the jeweler speak. "It was the flower you wanted to look at, right?"

"Yes, the flo—"

"Zac," I cut him off. It takes a moment before I glance back and flex my jaw side to side. "The treasure chest. You should look at the treasure chest."

He looks over his shoulder, perplexed. "Why?"

I lick my lips, remembering the most ridiculous secret that Summer shared with me once. "I don't know," I lie. "Just... the treasure chest is a nice pick."

Now I'm in Summer's house with my brother dead and a necklace around her neck that I knew would make her happy.

Rubbing my hands over my face, I'm beginning to wonder why I'm putting myself through this. I should just ignore my brother's request and move on.

But it's Summer.

And a baby that's my nephew.

If she truly needs someone to help her like everyone suggests then I'll never forgive myself, because before my brother would protect her, and now there is only me.

Summer saunters back into the living room, oblivious to my mind having just gone down memory lane.

"You don't get a choice. I'm just ordering pizza, going to steal a slice, and then I'll give Bo a bath, bottle, and everything. By the way, he can try soft foods in little pieces, just stay away from honey. I guess you'll learn quickly. Also, he likes going for 'swims.'" She uses air quotes. "At the Dizzy Duck. I know it's technically a spa pool, but Holden doesn't mind. The water is perfectly warm too. The other thing is Bo still wakes once a night, so be prepared for that." She's rambling again.

I grimace. "You're going to keep using his routine as our talking point, aren't you?"

She heaves a sigh because she's been called out. "Yeah," she answers bluntly. Summer climbs down to the floor and crosses her legs, getting comfortable as it seems she is willing to talk.

"We're out of our depth, Nash," she admits.

"We always were," I reflect.

"You're leaving in six weeks? Zac wanted six weeks."

I rub the back of my neck as I give a long exhale. "I don't know, probably. I can't think clearly."

Summer picks up a toy block that was on the floor within reach and begins to toss it between her hands. "You're bound to get close with Bo, so whatever you plan on doing, just remember you need to follow through. Don't just be an uncle for six weeks, play the long game."

I hold my palm up. "I understand."

She shakes her head in disbelief. "I don't trust you. We just need to look at history to know that you won't commit, and you always find a reason to stay away. But Nash..." Her warning turns sharp. "This isn't me. It's Bo, an innocent baby who is oblivious to life's heartaches. So don't you dare run away again."

I lift my nose slightly. "Are you really just talking on behalf of Bo?" I challenge, because underlying, she could mean her too.

She grumbles, clearly annoyed or wanting to escape the

truth as she is quick to scramble to her feet. "Discussion over."

I have my answer.

———

A FEW HOURS LATER, Summer and I haven't really crossed paths. Only when she showed me how to handle a diaper and bottle did she actually construct a sentence around me. When pizza came, she gobbled down a slice, and we again focused on Bo who makes a mess when tomato sauce and melted cheese are involved. Then again, he can't eat the crust yet.

Still, despite dinner, I'm searching the fridge, not exactly sure what I'm looking for. I'm restless and on edge that I'll run into Summer.

My theory is proven correct when I hear the soft patter of footsteps approaching the kitchen. Sighing, I close the fridge and prepare myself to see the beautiful woman that's tormented me for years, and it's all my fault.

Flicking my eyes up, I see that Summer slows her step, and her face shows caution, yet it's gentle. Why does she have to wear an off-the-shoulder t-shirt that displays the curve of her bare shoulder?

"Hi."

Folding my arms against my chest, I lean against the counter. "Hi," I reply.

Her fingers twist the hem of her shirt. "I'm not sure what to say to you when Bo isn't around. You and I have an edgy relationship to say the least."

Glancing to the side, I do my best to gather composure. "Well…" I click my tongue in my mouth.

A long silence feels as though we could take a knife and slice it.

Summer rolls her eyes. "Great talk." She's not impressed, and I'm unsure if it's us or me. Frustrated, she turns to pick up a dirty bottle with aggravation. Her insistence to use glass baby bottles is not the best of ideas because as she twists to head to the sink, she drops it and glass shatters on the floor. "Shit."

I'm quick to take a few steps and lean down at the same time as her. She's already picking up little pieces which makes zero sense as she will need a dustpan and brush for sure. Her movements are as sharp as the shards of glass.

Placing my hand on the back of her palm, she stills. "Slow down," I whisper. At last, her eyes swing up to pin her face in my view, but she says nothing. I can't help it. That little scar, it's part of her for life. "Does it hurt?"

She understands what I mean. Her lips press together. "No."

Licking my lips, I drop my head down and pick up a big piece of glass. "Who the hell still uses glass baby bottles?" I attempt to make a joke, but she's in no mood.

"A normal person who just decided that life is already a little fucked up, so might as well add a fragile baby bottle that's a pain to carry around as it leaks. But hey, points for me for finding the funny little things in this living arrangement," she counters.

Here we go.

"Why are you always so feisty?" I wonder.

Her death glare is a bullseye to my chest. "I'm only this way with you."

"Lucky me."

She's quick to keep this debate going. "It's not my fault my mouth has a mind of its own around you."

I smirk. "I know, I remember your mouth."

Her eyes turn into saucers because I just reminded her of

the fact that our bodies mold together with perfection, and we know exactly how to make one another see stars.

"Nice. Smug Nash is making an appearance tonight." Her sarcasm isn't appreciated.

"How about you just accept that I'm here." My voice has an edge.

"I'm trying," she grits out as our eyes stay locked.

"Could've fooled me." I whistle a sound.

Her tongue swipes along her teeth. "Are we just going to go back and forth?"

We both take a moment to sigh, and we collapse into sitting on the floor, completely exhausted from our little tit-for-tat.

Vulnerability kicks in. "I just want to do the right thing. I've only ever done what everyone needs."

She deflates and scoffs to herself. "What a lie. Then, you were only what I needed."

It surprises me that she admits that, and it twists my stomach. "But you're what he needed, and in the end, you have a son," I remind us.

Summer seems to grasp my theory, and she gulps a breath. "Can we just not talk about this anymore?"

"Agreed." I pick up a large piece of glass. "I'll clean this up."

"I can do it."

Now I have to laugh. "Let's not go down another spiral of arguing over stupid shit."

She bobs her head in agreement. "You're right."

Our eyes meet for a brief second. "Can I just do what I want to do? I'll take care of you. I'll clean this up. Anything else? A leaky pipe. Mowing the grass. There must be something."

Anything to occupy me from wanting to take care of her in other ways.

Her head tilts slightly to the side. "I mean… I guess the sink does have a drip."

"I'm on it," I promise.

The moment that she rolls her shoulder back and seems to ease sends a whoosh of relief down my body. "Actually, I really could use some help…" Her finger twirls in the air. "Babyproofing, the crawling phase will hit us at any moment."

Reaching out, I touch her wrist. "No problem. I'll be a pro at it and earn myself another point on the baby-experience scale."

Her eyes flood with appreciation and proof that I'm chipping away a piece of our wall. Summer nods once before her eyes drop down to soak in the view of my fingers connecting us. After a moment, she begins to teeter up. "Thanks. Uh, if you're okay with this," she indicates to the floor, "I'll go finish some laundry and things. I guess… I'll see you tomorrow."

"Sure."

We both seem to blow out a breath at the same time.

———

UPSTAIRS, I try to adjust to the fact that I'm in a guest room that has empty drawers and a closet. It's a nice room, a log cabin meets modern feel with a quilt on the bed. Zac and Summer seem to have good taste in interior design.

Summer kept to her word that she would be busy with Bo, and I've heard enough squeals from a baby with the sound of water running to calm any nerves.

But it is a momentary pause, because when the upstairs grows quiet, anxiousness reappears with a vengeance.

Summer's on the other side of the wall, sleeping, alone in bed, with her heart in pieces. She's strong, but even warriors need breaks.

Walking, I stop and reach up to plant a palm against the white wall, wondering what she's like on the other side.

Is she sleeping or lying with her gaze stuck on the ceiling because we're breathing the same air under the same roof, and that alone can cause an earthquake.

SUMMER

I'm more agitated than I should be today. While Bo slept like an angel, I barely slept a wink. Knowing Nash is on the other side of my bedroom wall will not be great for the lines under my eyes.

"So, how's it going with the brother-in-law? I'm beginning to wonder if you think he's from hell," Lexi asks casually as we walk down the hall of the inn toward the event room. She sometimes visits Holden during the day, but lately she's been decorating the place for fall and Halloween, as she's an interior designer.

My eyes slide up for a mere second then focus again on my list of upcoming events. "Fine. Barely. Okay. Whatever."

She stunts a laugh. "Sounds peachy."

I sigh and give up on trying to work and drop the list, and it hangs by my side in my clasp. "I'm trying to adapt to this whirlwind that my late husband seemed to have insisted he throw my way as a parting gift." Cynicism is my coping method.

"Makes sense. It's just you seem completely, well, almost… I can't pinpoint it, but it's a mix of good and bad."

She reviews me then extends her palm up. "I mean, you have total right to feel every emotion under the sun lately."

I throw her a glare because she knows not to treat me like delicate goods. She gawks at me at the reminder.

"Sorry," she apologizes before she presses the button on her watch. "Shit. Sorry to cut this short, but I need to meet the PTA moms for planning a fundraiser."

Ah, I needed to hear that because it makes me burst out with a laugh. "I can't believe you actually had a campaign to be voted head of the PTA."

"There's no shame in using cupcakes and bottles of wine to sway the vote," she defends.

"It's just… I can only imagine what they all think of you. The hot younger stepmom who infiltrated their circle."

Lexi shrugs. "They needed a new direction. Their former committee president wasn't upping her game in school events and was being a total bitch to half the population."

That whole situation has been fun to see. She loves Holden's kids like they're her own, because sometimes a parent comes in many forms. It causes a thought in my head, wondering if Nash will have this sort of feeling with Bo one day in the absence of Zac. The moment I process what I just imagined, I shake it off.

"Oh, hey." Harlow approaches us, and she looks as though she's heading to the gym.

"Bye, you guys, gotta run," Lexi greets her and scurries away.

My smile remains, and Harlow looks over her shoulder and her thumb directs toward Lexi who is turning a corner. "Another kid crisis?"

"Something like that." She hums a sound in understanding. "What brings you here?"

"Wanted to walk on the treadmill and use some tiny

weights to stay in shape." She glances down at her protruding belly. "Besides, Stone wanted to meet with Holden and your new houseguest apparently. A Dizzy Duck executive meeting."

I stand in attention. "Oh."

Crap. I must look uncomfortable with the information that she's brought to light.

"Is that a problem?"

I bite my bottom lip as she observes me peculiarly.

Assessing the area, I decide mornings are sometimes too quiet here. That's the tranquility of Lake Spark, right? Guess it's a good time for a sounding board. "Hey, can I ask you something?"

"Of course."

I draw my tongue along my lip and tap the nails of my free hand against my dark fitted jeans. The perks of working at a boutique hotel is we can wear what we want within reason.

"Have you ever, I don't know, thought or known something, and as much as you want to keep it to yourself, you know you shouldn't? But if you do, then it can kind of turn the tide of daily life?"

Harlow exhales deeply and offers me an empathetic look. "I have." I'm an idiot, of course she has; past life events that she doesn't share often because they are just plain horrendous.

"What did you do?" I ask.

"Well, I wanted to keep it in more than anything. It took a while, but then I shared it with someone."

My neck elongates. "And?"

"It all became easier. Life became easier."

My entire body eases from the reality of what I already

knew but needed confirmation on. "I was afraid you might say that."

"Then what's stopping you?"

"A further complication that it could cause," I reply.

Her eyes still appraise me, and she reaches out to my shoulder in comfort. "But will it really?"

"Haven't figured that out yet," I admit.

"Deep down you know. A moment will present itself."

"Maybe so."

I know so.

———

"HERE, LET ME DO IT." I take over the mouse for the laptop from Stuart as we stand behind the receptionist desk. "Just click here then pull up the reservation screen." My actions follow my words as we attempt to tackle the new software.

"I don't think that helps," he points out.

I grumble and begin to jab the mouse button repeatedly to no avail.

"Go easy, will ya?" Holden says as he approaches the desk.

My eyes dart up to find Holden with a smile walking next to Nash who has an unreadable expression.

I grumble slightly. "Sorry. I'm just..." Nope. Not going to admit that I'm tired. "Forgot to grab my cup of coffee," I lie.

Nash clears his throat. "I can grab you one if you want."

"I don't need you to save the day," I mutter with annoyance, but then everyone darts their attention to me because they heard.

"Well... that's our cue to leave you two. Come on, Stuart, I think a new box of wine bottles arrived," Holden suggests, and in my side view, I can see Stuart give an odd look and nod in agreement.

It takes a few seconds, but then Nash and I stare at one another, and we're both unsure who should say something first.

It's me. "I forgot that you suddenly have an interest in the hotel." At least my normal voice is back.

"Yeah, thought I would have a meeting with Holden first thing after a run."

I swallow. "I would say that I noticed you gone this morning, but I'm used to having no house guests, so it was a normal morning," I fib. I actually assumed it was avoidance.

"Right, I forgot to ask about the childcare situation with Bo when you're at work." Nash runs his hand along the back of his neck.

My cheeks rise as I laugh silently to myself. "You did mention that your baby skills were a two out of ten, so I'm not surprised." It causes him to ease. "My neighbor's eighteen-year-old daughter mostly watches him since she's taking night classes at the community college."

"Okay. Uhm, just let me know if you need me to watch him."

I'm now entertained. "Are you sure? Because you sound unsure."

He licks his lips that I remember as powerful. "It's why I'm here, isn't it? I want to help. I'll just need to pick up a few baby-whisperer abilities. That's all."

I tap my nails on the desk, debating what to do. I need to make this easier on us, except it probably won't. In fact, I'm about to lead us down a dangerous road.

I skim the lobby with my eyes and see that there is one older guest who is enjoying his cup of coffee while reading a financial newspaper as he sits in a comfortable chaise lounge.

Tucking a few loose strands of my hair behind my ear, I take the plunge. "Perhaps we can talk outside?" I suggest.

"Sure." Nash seems invested in wanting to have a discussion which is a start.

I close the laptop on the desk, perhaps with a little too much gusto. Nash lifts his arm out, indicating that I should lead the way. I offer him a polite half-smile, and he follows me in tow.

Just like the other day, we find ourselves on the inn's dock. And again, we face one another in an odd silence. I glance down at my foot as I draw a half circle on the wood, and I cross my arms.

Nash stuffs his hands into the pockets of his jeans as he rocks on his heels. "We always seem to end up here… past and present."

Our eyes meet with recognition. "Seems so." We linger in a moment that feels too heavy on my chest. "We should probably get over this awkwardness if we're going to be around one another more."

Nash nods once. "I agree."

"We have both been thrown into an unknown realm that Zac set us in."

He scoffs. "He was your husband. You would know him best."

That sets me off like a cannonball. "You really are going to keep throwing it in my face, aren't you? That I had a husband and have a son. And it's with your brother, too."

"Sorry." There is remorse in his tone, and he rubs his forehead.

"I'm not sure that's true." I mosey on past him with my back now facing him. "You're the one who walked away all those years ago. You had me first then let go."

"And you walked straight into his arms." Now he just sounds bitter again.

I pivot, and my head whips in his direction. "*You* paved the road, Nash." Anger is now building up. I walk straight to him and push him because I'm furious at the heartache he gave me. "Maybe Zac never realized, but you're the one who pushed me away because of loyalty to your brother. I know I'm right."

"At least someone got their wish." His words are barely audible but not quiet enough. "He got you. The whole reason I let you go. He got the wife who he loved because you moved on from me."

I growl in frustration. "You wanted this!" I jostle him again.

He tenses, and he too is aggravated but does his best to keep it in. "Summer," he cautions.

I step in again, and he steps back. "No. I won't walk around as though I've done something wrong by becoming a wife and a mother."

Nash looks away. "A part of me always thought that you wouldn't return his feelings, but still, we couldn't hurt him. I just didn't think you two would ever happen. But he actually got to put a ring around your finger."

My shoulders puff up, and I do my best to square off with him. "Nash, you have no clue, do you?"

His brows rise. "What? That you were his wife and had a baby with Zac? It's pretty obvious."

My hands form fists as my tongue swipes across my teeth, gathering my strength for this conversation. "I loved him but in a different way."

He shakes his head, not believing me.

"Nash, I wanted to make him happy while he was sick. He asked, and I didn't say no because that's how much I care for him, but that doesn't mean that I was madly in love, you idiot."

His entire body stills as if a bullet just hit him, and for a few ticks, he evaluates my words. "Say that again."

"Our marriage wasn't what you thought."

Nash voluntarily steps back, and my feet follow as I face him, but it causes him to stumble… right into the water.

"Nash!"

The sound of water splashing and the sight of Nash's head appearing above water as he slows his strokes has me instantly near the edge.

I lean down and offer my hand which is ridiculous, as he's too strong for me anyhow. "This wasn't how this conversation was supposed to go."

"Really? Wouldn't have thought." He's sarcastic but reaches up for my hand.

In a flash, he curls his hand around my wrist and yanks me, causing me to lose my balance and plunge into the water with him.

What the hell? Now I'm furious all over again.

I flail my arms until I find stillness. My nipples are hard as pebbles, and I'm already freezing. I'm completely soaked, and my makeup is probably melting down my skin.

"Are you crazy?" I yell. "It's the end of September and the water is cold."

"Oh yeah? Then why did you cause me to fall in?"

I'm stunned. "Are you serious? You tripped!"

"Because you just casually mentioned something quite key to this little set-up my brother has thrown me into." Nash sounds livid.

"Ugh, I'm reminded why I think that I might hate you."

He swims closer to me. "Maybe I hate you too, except

you know, that I never could, and I'm sure you know the sentiment."

"Fine! I dislike you with a strong dose of anger."

He pushes water toward me. "Ditto, Summer."

I splash water at him, frustrated. "Well, now you know. I married Zac when he told me he was sick and he had a wish. He was my best friend, something felt right about it. I cared so deeply for him, and I knew he loved me. I'd already been feeling alone for some time, and then he asked. I was over-whelmed."

Nash's nostrils flare. "Why didn't you clue me the fuck in about your marriage situation?"

"Really? That's your concern? You weren't at the top of the list of who to inform. Because if I recall, you sure as hell weren't dropping by for weekly family dinners or expressing an interest that you would come crawling back to me."

"I had hockey, and I had to stay away from y—" He cuts his statement short.

I growl as my legs whirl underneath the water. "Well, I made sure that happened. Besides, some things made sense between Zac and me. We were friends who made one another happy. Just not…"

Deeply in love.

"And Bo?"

"Sue me. We did something a few times, and maybe it was even an unspoken compromise because I've always wanted to be a mom. We ended up with a great child, your nephew."

Nash blinks as everything sinks in, literally.

Now that he knows this, everything is more dangerous between Nash and me.

We shouldn't be around one another. But right now, our

bodies are nearly pressed together because I take hold of his shirt.

"Why the fuck did you have you to tell me this?" He nearly sneers.

"What?" My voice squeaks as I look up the sky because now I think Nash is crazy.

"This tidbit of information might have been useful." He's flippant. "Especially when deciding to stay here."

Because it makes it all even more complicated.

I shake my head and shove water his way. "No shit."

He continues to swim in place, clearly agitated. "You are not on the list of people who make me feel okay right now."

"I'm sure your list is non-existent on a normal day."

"Fuck," he barks. "I had the tiniest inclinations that your relationship might have been something like this. I just didn't want the fucking confirmation." He slams his hands on top of the water causing more ripples on the surface.

"What the hell does that mean?" My voice raises an octave.

Nash's eyes laser in, and he looks at me as if I should solve the riddle. "It might make it hurt even more."

I shake my head. "If you rewind the last five minutes, then you would realize we've established that it's *you* who led us all down this path."

"The past few days you let me think that your marriage was…"

"We started on the wrong foot because you're still a cocky asshole sometimes."

Nash growls then wipes droplets from his face. "The house?" His cheeks rise, and he's trying to keep his temper down.

"Oh, you mean which room I made a baby in?" I mock him, and it only makes him more dismayed.

"Summer," he grits out a warning.

I glance away then slide my eyes back to him. "I only moved in with Bo when Zac was in the hospital. So to answer your very inappropriate question from the other day, no. No, there is not a room where I made a baby in my house. The bed is new, too, you asshole. And while we're at it, no. No, I never told him about us. I made a promise, and I tend to keep those." I'm nearly livid that we're discussing this topic.

Nash stares at me blankly. "Okay," he replies with zero indication of what's running through his mind.

"Oh gee, does my answer appease you? I really want to throttle you right now."

He peers down and back up with a faint chuckle. "Well, you could if you want. Look where we are."

I take a moment to let the surroundings remind me of my setting. "Shit. Why are we still in the water?"

"Because you felt the need to explain important facts here," he says, irritated.

I growl. "Ugh, I need to find a way to live with you. This is ridiculous that I'm in the lake."

He smirks at me, and it's so smug. I remember that look. The one he would give before his mouth would move lower on my body. "What's even more ludicrous is that we can stand here."

"What?" *Oh.* It's a bit of a reach, but still, my feet touch the bottom of the lake and my head is still above the water.

Then it happens as we both stand. A calmness overtakes us as we stare at one another. A moment where even I can let my mouth ease into a small smile. It's not every day that you can clear the air in cold water. The corners of his mouth stretch up because he must feel it too.

Nash's hand comes out on offer. "A peace offering? No more jabs at one another?"

I think for a moment then sigh. Bo shouldn't be dragged into Nash's and my history. "Yes."

Reluctantly, I slide my hand into his. The connection hits with a jolt and an anger that the water on our skin is an extra layer between us. It rushes through my body, the patter of my heart and the warning that a truth may alter the moments that I'm alone with Nash.

But I won't think too hard as I walk up the slant of the dark sand on the shore.

We both look up to see that we have an entire audience.

Holden's face is puzzled. "Uh… you guys okay? I thought about throwing in the life vest, but when we all heard you two screaming that you hate one another, we decided you have some issues to work out."

While Nash continues his slow walk with a satisfied grin, I look at Holden and a few other staff members with embarrassment.

"How much of that did you hear?" I wonder.

"Nothing except the hate part. Kind of concerning," Holden tells me, pretty amused by all of this.

I hold my hand up, and my breath is heavy. "I think this…" I twirl a finger in the air, "is my cue that I might need to leave early today. I'm freezing, and I think…" I blink, trying to adapt to being back on land.

Holden holds his palms up. He's trying to suppress a laugh. "Say no more."

"What? What was that?" Nash cups his ear with his hand, pretending to try and listen. "Pick up milk from the grocery store since we now have a truce and I need to up my baby-whispering game from a two? You got it."

A rumbling sound rolls up my throat.

Was this a turning point for us? Arguing in the water to have transparency about our current situation…

…except our situation just became more complex. We now have a new kind of tension.

NASH

I sit quietly at the kitchen table with a beer bottle in hand, doing my best to run through the facts that I've learned. Truthfully, I don't know how to process it all. I don't doubt that Summer and Zac had their own kind of relationship. One that, if I'm honest with myself, gave my brother solace before he passed.

It's just, now I'm under the same roof as Summer and wondering what happens when we bury the past and start on a fresh page, if we can.

The sound of feet walking down the stairs doesn't snap me out of my subdued mood. Hearing Summer's steps slow doesn't change the feeling, either. Still, my eyes flick up to watch her delicately enter the kitchen as she dries her hair with a towel.

"Hi."

I take one sip of my beer. "Hey."

Our eyes meet, and it feels like we have reached a gate with each of us on opposite sides. Summer swipes her hair to the side, and her small scar confronts me the way it always does when I least expect.

"So… that was that." She's trying to approach the subject.

It causes me to smirk slightly to myself. "What can I say? That dock does stupid shit to people. Some weird possessed sacred piece of wood over water."

"That's one way of looking at it." She slides onto a chair and pulls her knee up to wrap her arms around her leg. "I'm sorry."

"For what, Summer?"

She seems to brace herself. "That we ended up in Lake Spark. There was probably a better way to have discussed this all."

My shoulders lift. "It is what it is."

"Some days, I don't even know how to process the last two years. It's a lot."

My lips wrap around my beer bottle for another sip, but beer is doing fuck all to simmer me down. "You did what you felt was right, and you have a son that makes you happy."

Warmth washes over her face. "He does." It's a long moment of silence as our sight stakes the other. "You and I called a ceasefire."

"So we did." And I have zero clue how non-angry us will be.

Her eyes seem to wander around as her fingers tap on the table. "We should probably break the ice again… between us, I mean."

I laugh to myself. "And how do you propose we do that?"

"Hmm…" Her eyes catch on something. "How about we play a boardgame?"

Now I have to smile at her absurd suggestion. "A boardgame?"

"Yeah. We have a bunch. Remember, your brother had a whole collection? We also have the old-school game system, but that's in a box somewhere."

She stands and eagerly finds her way to a cupboard against the wall. There are a bunch of candles on top of what looks to be a refurbished antique dresser. She opens the door, and her finger taps her chin. "I know. We can honor Zac by playing one of his favorite games. That boardgame where it's like medieval times. There are like three different boxes, I guess for new levels or new kingdoms or something weird like that."

A chuckle booms out of me. "Oh man, I think I know where this is going. Open the lid and I'll have my answer."

Her face is etched in curiosity, and she peeks down as she opens the game. "Oh no, hell no." Now my head lolls to the side, and I grin to myself. "It's like a gazillion pieces. Cards, little figures, is that more figures but in different sizes?" She tips her head to the side to examine the contents. "This must take like an hour to set up."

"So that's a no?" I press.

Summer looks at me, horrified, before she closes the box again and sets it back in the cupboard. "We should probably stick to cards. That's simple."

Then my body stills again. "Cards," I state, and my lips roll into my mouth.

It registers in her head. "Right. Cards." This can't keep happening. "We always used to play with Zac when we were teenagers…"

I say nothing.

"And when I was upset that my parents were divorcing during my last year of high school and I showed up to see Zac, my best friend, he wasn't there, but you were…"

I stand and take a few steps when I see a shade of pain, though it's not because of me. It's because it makes her think of Zac, except laced with conflict. I touch her shoulder with my fingertips. "It's okay, he won't be angry if you remember memories of you and me, or at least, that's what I choose to tell myself, now."

Her face softens when she looks at me, and she nods once in understanding. "I didn't want to be alone. My brother was already about to finish college."

I interrupt her. "Your brother always hated me, I'm sure of it."

Summer snickers a laugh. "Keats? Well, maybe." That's a yes. Her face softens, with her eyes tipping up to meet my gaze. "Your parents were away, and we played cards. We kissed for the first time, and you held me while I was upset, and we slept in your bed. It was a blip, easy to forget and never act on again, a little secret but doable. Then years later, we discovered we were wrong."

I remain composed. "Despite what happened down the road, it's a bittersweet memory, and I'm not sure that's so bad."

Her pressed lips stretch in my favor. "You're right." But it takes only a few seconds for Summer to create space and begin to busy herself. I watch her as she ties up her hair, the slope of her neck taunting me. "You know, I think I forgot to get more oatmeal. Bo likes that with a little jam. I should find my keys and go to the grocery store."

"Oh, yeah, totally," I answer dryly.

She begins to walk in the direction of the living room but stalls and snaps her fingers in the air. "Shit. The neighbor will drop Bo off soon. I should probably…"

I step forward. "It's fine. I'm here, and surely, I can handle that." It's clear that she needs some air and a moment away from the house.

She gives me an appreciative smile. "Okay, let's consider it your trial on baby skills, except there can be no error."

My cheeks rise from her humor that is blossoming back. "Noted."

"Won't be long."

I nod and watch her walk out the door. Except, in a little while, she'll walk right back in.

———

"SERIOUSLY? It's an entire toy with many popping animal options, and you just want to focus on the lion for the hundredth time?" I tell my nephew as he sits up, continuing to press the button with the animal appearing before he closes the square again. Every time his giggle causes me to smile wider.

I've never really thought about kids in my life. It's not that I'm against it. It just never got that serious with any woman that I've dated. My brother always wanted a wife, kids, dog, and a home that was more than just a house. Me? I guess I was still figuring it all out.

Bo lets out a yawn, and I feel like it's a cue that at last the toy can take a rest. "Come on, buddy. Someone mentioned that you sleep a lot, and I'm not sure you're supposed to sleep before dinner, so let's just chill a little, okay?"

I pick him up in my arms and carry him to the sofa. Getting comfortable, I rest him against my chest, throw my feet up on the table—even though Summer hates it—and grab the nearby remote control to turn the television on to head straight to the sports channel. "A little hockey highlights to prepare you for your future."

My companion doesn't answer, and when I look down, I see him struggling to keep his eyes open, with his lids hooding closed.

It must be a little later when my eyes slowly open, and I

realize that I must have dozed off, and I feel a warm weight against my chest. Glancing down, my nephew is asleep even with the TV still on as background noise. In my peripheral view, I notice Summer watching as she leans against the frame of the wall where the living room joins the kitchen. Her arms are clasping her long sweater tightly, and her ankles are crossed; it doesn't feel as though she just arrived.

Lifting my head, I do my best not to move so my nephew doesn't wake. "Hey, how long have you been there?"

Her mouth tugs. "Long enough." It translates to she's been observing us. "Seems you upgraded from a two to a four on the baby-experience scale."

My stunted laugh is scratchy and groggy. "Good to know."

Summer quietly walks to us and leans down to coax him awake. "As much as Bo is in his zone in dreamland, I'm going to wake him up to ensure he sleeps during the night. Otherwise, none of us will get shuteye."

Her hand snakes under him and against my chest to try and lift him up. The space between all of us is far too close. Summer's long hair feathers my arm as she scoops up Bo. The moment she is standing with her son resting his head against her shoulder and her hand swirling on his back, I feel alone.

She begins to sway as he stirs. "He's a cuddler. It's nearly impossible to just lie with him, you'll always join him on his nap."

I sit up and stretch. "I have now experienced the proof."

"I didn't think about dinner when I was at the store," she mentions.

I grimace. "Probably because you didn't go to the store."

Her eyes travel the room to avoid me and hide her pressed smile. "Very true. A drive around the lake it was."

I stand and choose not to begin an inquest on how her time for air was or if it helped. "What do you want for dinner?"

"Oh, I'll probably just make a sandwich or something."

My eyes narrow. "Is that really dinner?"

With Bo now more awake, she bounces him gently. "Well, I normally don't cook. I don't really have time, and it's just easier since I'm alon—" She ends her admission because Summer probably thinks I'm going to judge.

"Alone?" I finish the sentence for her.

"Something like that. Just seems silly, that's all. Besides, I'm so busy with Bo that I think I forget half the time," she confesses, but as soon as she realizes, a sound pulls from her throat. "I mean…"

I raise my palm to calm her. "Relax. I'm not judging you or taking this as a point that you need someone to watch out for you like everyone seems to want," I partly lie. I'm not going to use this as ammo, but I'm not thrilled with the fact that she takes care of herself last. Bo is resilient and happy, but that doesn't mean that Summer can't follow suit.

Summer rolls her lips in, aware that I'm right.

I clap my hands together. "I've learned to cook…" Her eyes widen, and she seems impressed. "No other option when I was playing pro. Had to watch the nutrients. Anyhow, we'll save your taste-testing for another night. I'll run to the deli to pick up some meals they have. Pasta, chicken?"

Summer's eyes flutter. "Oh, I…" Then her stance turns confident. "Sure. Thanks." Her genuine smile looks good on her. It's honest.

"No problem."

"Do you think you can stop by the drugstore? They were out of Bo's bath soap, it's this special kind of natural stuff I get. They ordered some more the other day, and it should be in now."

I salute her. "I will complete my mission."

"Thanks."

"Sure."

Our eyes struggle to break apart. It's these long lingering moments that are not good for us. No wonder she fled earlier to get air.

———

I'M WAITING PATIENTLY while the older man behind the counter searches in the back for Summer's order. My eyes wander around as there is something quaint about Lake Spark in that everything is a throwback to another era. My sight lands on the wall of jars that are filled with candy that you put in a bag then they weigh at the end. It always made my grandmother give us stories about when she was younger. Zac and I would always listen then wrap her around our finger to get caramel toffees. Young us were charmers and were such a team.

"Summer Nix?"

For a moment my heart flurries from the sound of that name and how my last name sounds good on her. But then my heart drops when I have to remind myself that she has the name because of my brother.

I scratch the back of my head. "Yeah, that's her." He hands me the bag with a post-it attached, and I clear my throat. "Uhm, yeah, thank you."

"No problem." He smiles brightly at me, and I give him a curt nod.

I'm quick to leave, and when I'm out the door, my phone vibrates in my pocket. Balancing the bag and swiping my screen when I see it's my mom calling, I answer.

"Hey, Mom," I say, unsure if today she is doing better than the others. My parents are also finding a routine again since Zac's passing. It's just, I can't help feeling that when they talk to me, it stirs everything up. I'm the other son. The one who is alive and for the most part well. It's especially my dad who is quite cold with me.

"Hi, Nash. Just wanted to check in." She sounds as though today is a good day for her, which is a relief.

"No need to check in," I remind her as I continue to walk toward my car on Main Street.

She lets out a breath. "How is she? Bo?"

Ah, that's why she's really calling. "They're… they're fine. Bo seems happy. He's a baby, after all."

"That's nice. He's growing fast from what I see from the photos that Summer sends. We're planning a time to come up and visit. And Summer? How is she holding up?"

A sting hits my body. How do I say she's thriving if I'm not quite sure it's the truth? I'm sure as hell not going to say that she's keeping herself so damn occupied that I'm beginning to think she's running herself thin. Or that me being in Lake Spark only stirs things that shouldn't be touched.

"She's doing the best she can for Bo." That's not a lie, at least.

"I'm happy to hear. You be sure to help them out while you're in town. Your brother would have wanted that. He held Summer and Bo so close to his heart."

I swallow because my parents have no clue the dynamics between Summer and Zac. Let alone when I'm thrown into the equation.

"I know, Mom."

"I'm actually calling because I need you to check on the

house. The realtor wants to take photos next week as we prepare to put the house on the market. But I would like you to run through to see if anything needs to be fixed or seems out of place."

A grin curves on my mouth. "Would it matter? The size of the house makes up for anything that could be wrong. I'm sure it will sell fast." Kind of a shame, too. It's a great house full of memories.

"Maybe you're right. Also…"

"Yes?"

She stalls for a second or two. "Your brother left you a box. He had set some things aside before… well, he wanted to ensure we saved some things for Bo. I guess he found stuff from when you guys were younger. I set the box in the den before we left to head south."

Yet again today, I pause in my step before I reach my car. "Oh. I didn't realize he did that." Probably because I vanished after he passed.

"He loved you a lot."

"Zac was special." That's why I let him have his gift that ended up being his wife and giving him a son.

"Mmhmm."

I sigh. "I'll check on the house, maybe on my way home. Have to run some errands."

"Thanks, sweetie."

Ending the call, I close my eyes for a second to adjust to the fact that I saw him less in recent years when he needed a brother more than anything. Yet, my brother did a kind gesture by leaving me mementos when he deserved more from me.

Still, I get in my car and throw the bag of baby shampoo on the front seat. It's early, and I figure we have another hour before it's dinner time. Or rather, Summer can eat after Bo goes to bed, so she doesn't need to rush dinner.

My drive around the lake with changing leaves doesn't do much for clearing my head. Nor does arriving to my childhood home. After parking, entering the security code, and walking into the hall, I do a quick assessment of the place. I know they still have a cleaner visit every other week and a lawn service for the yard. There isn't much to check on, as everything is the way it should be.

That may be a stretch. The house is missing people inside who are happy, far from aching.

Remembering that there is a box waiting for me because our lives are in mourning, I enter the den where memories trickle into my thoughts. The way Zac would game or have friends over to watch TV and plan BBQs. He and I would watch movies. Summer would join us, and there was always popcorn being thrown. They were always good times.

I spot the box on the sofa, and I'm not nervous to open it. Maybe I should be. Lifting the lid off, I instantly snort a laugh. My eyes are greeted with a game system and collection of his old-school games. Summer wasn't wrong about it being in a box somewhere. There is also a trophy that our friends got us because we apparently committed the best prank on the history teacher on Halloween. A pack of cards that we would always play when we would visit our grandparents. A plastic Easter egg because we got roped into manning the Easter egg hunt at the Dizzy Duck when I was sixteen.

I pick up more things from what would appear to be a box of junk but is anything but. One by one, a flood of happiness washes over me. His notebook of drawings, feeling like it's a piece of art even though it's mostly nonsense. I toss it to the side.

Everything is out when I notice one last thing at the bottom of the box. An envelope of photos with the seal broken, and I have a peek at the few, mostly family photos and Zac and me at a party together. One more that's Summer, Zac, and me. Different to the one on Summer's living room mantle. I turn the pictures for dates. Memory lane suddenly steals my breath, with my entire body experiencing its own clap of thunder.

A date is a reminder of how time passes.

I wave the photo against my palm. I'm not sure now is the time to recap to myself that time passing can also equate to wearing off and making room for a revival or change.

And for now, I just want to get on with my day.

––––––

I SET the food on the kitchen counter. It's just rotisserie chicken and a few sides from the deli. Figured, there would be leftovers for tomorrow. A quick glance at the oven clock and it's already time for when Summer must be almost done with Bo's nighttime routine, so I decide to let her know that dinner is ready since the chicken just came out of the rotisserie at the store and is still warm.

I jog up the stairs but halt when I arrive at the top because I hear a sniffle. Teetering on my feet, I slowly approach Bo's nursery, and with the door partly ajar with only the nightlight on, I can see that he's asleep.

Summer? She's standing over the crib and watching him, wiping her tears away.

She must hear me because her head lifts gently in my direction, and she quickly smears a tear with the back of her hand along her cheek then takes a few paces to the door, silently stepping out, only to turn her back to me to pull the door closed.

My hand comes up to rest on her shoulder. "You okay?"

Her body melts into my hand that suddenly feels heavy.

"Fine. Just dust or something."

I encourage her to turn around and face me, and even though I succeed, her sight hangs low. "If that's what you want me to believe then I'll play along, but something tells me this happens a lot."

"Can we not make a deal out of this?" she quietly requests.

I blow out a breath. "If that's what you want, even though bullshit isn't my style."

Her puffy eyes give me attention. "It's not a daily occurrence if that's what you're thinking."

"Of course not, you dust the house every other day."

She appreciates my attempt to turn her sad moment around, but the quarter of a smile quickly wilts, her chin trembling instead. Summer steps forward, and my body reacts by bringing my arms up and engulfing her as she dives her face into my chest.

A hug.

That's what we find ourselves in.

She creates the barest of inches between my chest and her mouth, only to mumble, "I'm not sure if I'm sad that Zac is gone or… you're back, and I wonder too much what it all would've been like if our road were different long ago between you and me." More tears fall. "Does that make me a horrible person?"

I think I needed to hear her say that. I'm not alone. From instinct, I'm quick to wrap my arms around her and pull her tight to my body. Every bit of distance that I've attempted to keep between us over the years vanishes, and it feels as though a key turned.

"Don't ever think that." I kiss the top of her head, wanting with everything in my body to protect her from another cry that may escape.

"It hurts," she mutters before burying her head once more into my chest.

This is where she is supposed to be. That makes *me* the horrible person, because it's all I can think about. That she's supposed to be in my arms when she's in mourning for my brother.

But now isn't the time to explore my confliction.

"Today you forgot to dust it seems."

She chortles because apparently that loosens her down a level. "It was laundry day. I was too busy putting your ugly proboscis monkey stuffed animal in the washing machine," she quips.

Now I smile out all of my emotion. "You still have your wit, it seems. Come on, you need to eat. We're not really debating that, either."

Our eyes meet and they say enough.

Turns out we may just be able to support one another together.

A far cry from arguing in the lake.

SUMMER

The heaviness of sleep begins to fade as I stretch my body, my eyes blinking open. It takes a second or two, but then I realize where I am. In my bed, except I'm lying on top of the duvet with a throw blanket over my body. The setup causes me to sit up and attempt to recall how I got here.

The only thing that makes sense is that Nash must have carried me up here. I only remember sitting on the couch while he put away dishes. I must have fallen asleep. I rub my eyes to wake up further.

A little gesture begins to cause chaos inside of me. If I ended up here, then it means I was in *his* arms. For a moment, I let down my defenses yesterday, and a natural hug found my body far too close to his. The idea of Nash carrying me to my bedroom shouldn't affect me, but it does.

I hear the breakout of Bo's cry beginning to form. Our clocks are aligned, so I know that he is waking, too. I swing my legs out of bed, my feet touching the rug. I'm still in my tank top and jeans from yesterday, but I'll worry about that later.

Walking groggily into the hall, a peculiar sound occurs; Bo hasn't reached his full-fledged crying status.

My eyes open wide when I reach the doorway to his room. Immediately, my sight strikes up to the ceiling, trying to gain composure.

"Hey," Nash greets me.

He's pulling Bo up and out of his crib. Albeit, shirtless. What's worse is that I don't think he is even lacking a shirt on purpose. That just makes this all the more endearing.

Internally I curse to myself before getting a grip. "Hey. Looks like we can upgrade your baby skills from a four to a five." I meander into the room and reach my arms out to take hold of my son, but Nash makes no effort to hand him to me.

"It's good. I think I can handle making oatmeal if you want to change."

Subconsciously, my eyes slip down to examine myself, and I cross my arms as if I can shield myself. "Yeah, sure… uhm, thanks?" My voice is uneven. "I mean for taking me to bed." His eyes widen. Shit. "I mean not *to bed*, just bed, my bed, setting me in bed so I can sleep." Phew, I think I saved that.

He tries to suppress his melting grin, but I see it all the same. "I got what you meant the first time."

I blow out a breath, thankful that we can move on. "Just thanks. Okay?"

"No problem," Nash says as he swings his body side to side, and Bo seems to take interest in grabbing Nash's chin.

"And, yeah, that would help if you can do the oatmeal. I normally make it then bring him to the bathroom so I can shower and he chills in his bouncer," I explain.

I take a few steps to Bo's dresser and pull out some clothes and a fresh diaper then pause when I pivot to look at Nash with doubt. "Maybe I should get him dressed."

Nash chuckles. "Nah, I have to learn."

Skeptically, I agree. A few seconds' pause is mindless. Well, that is until it bursts out of my mouth about logistics last night. "How did you carry me up the stairs?"

He gives me a proud look. "Summer, I've played hockey most of my life. If I don't have the ability to carry you, then I think they were paying millions to the wrong person," he jokes.

It causes me to smirk. "If you say so."

Our eyes remain locked for a moment before I leave him to be with my son who is cooing.

The moment I'm out of the room, I lean against the hallway wall and sigh, acknowledging that there has been a shift between Nash and me. And it's scary.

———

WATCHING Nash skate is somehow soothing, with his hockey stick in hand, oblivious to me. Is it the sound of blades on ice? Or simply knowing that he'll be surprised I'm here.

Truthfully, I'm not exactly sure what possessed me to drive here, but my feet are planted to watch as I hold Bo in my arms. When Nash looks up for a millisecond, he does a double take, surprised that I'm here, as he should be. I raise Bo's wrist to give a little wave to Nash, and a faint line on his mouth slides up.

Nash slowly skates our way until he's at gate from the ice.

"Hey. Wasn't expecting you to be here."

My eyes circle the arena. "Well, me neither, but here I am. You mentioned earlier about coming here." My face must show that I'm pleased to be here; no jabs are planned to leave my mouth in the next few minutes.

Nash uses his stick to toss up the puck until he snatches it away and shows Bo. "Maybe you'll like hockey one day," he says to my son before his eyes dart to me as he waits for an explanation.

"I just wanted to… well, everyone is right, maybe." There I said it.

His face screws up in confusion.

"Maybe I do need a little help," I admit. Nash listens patiently. "Can we just forget I said anything." I'm backtracking and press my lips together and rinse the thoughts in my mind. But Nash's eyes study me, and his face is neutral. "Fine." I roll my eyes, caving. "Maybe we can just… keep it between us?"

"We're good at that," he remarks simply. My lashes bat as I recognize the truth in that. "But yeah… we can."

Appreciation floods my face.

"Anything for you," he mutters. I don't think he expected me to hear, but my breath hitches all the same.

"Lie of the century," I rasp. *He left.* "But let's keep this a normal conversation. Besides, there are seven-year-olds about the descend onto the ice. We can keep it classy and get an award for this perfectly normal conversation." I straighten my posture as much as I can with a baby propped on one hip.

The corners of his mouth twist. "Sure."

"Okay, well, uh… see you at home." He looks at me strangely, probably because I'm being awkward. Even when I turn to leave only to backtrack, I find him waiting in the exact spot with the exact same facial expression. "Actually, I thought about going for a coffee or ice cream with Bo. Maybe…"

Now he just grins. "I would like to tag along?" He helps me out because my invitation just spewed out of my mouth without thought.

"Yeah, something like that. Or like that." It drags out of my mouth.

He chuckles as he lowers his hand to unlock the gate. "I'll see you soon then."

———

DEBATING, I'm not sure if this is the right move. It's just Bo, and Nash is his uncle. I can't keep Nash at bay. This is good for Bo. Hence, why all three of us are wandering down Main Street to Jolly Joe's for ice cream.

"I'm surprised it isn't colder. The weather for fall seems to be okay," Nash remarks.

I continue to push Bo's stroller. "You may have jinxed us."

The fall decorations of Lake Spark overpower the scene. Pumpkins, hay bales, a weird-looking scarecrow, plus fakes leaves in shop windows.

"Are you decorating the house for Halloween?"

Shrugging a shoulder, I remind myself that is another item on my to-do list. "I guess I should at least get a pumpkin or something. Trick-or-treaters are ruthless here."

A brimming smile is pasted on his face. "Oh, I remember. Prime prank time."

"Speaking from experience." I give him a pointed look, very well aware of his younger antics.

"Don't you want to take Bo to a pumpkin patch or something? Isn't that a photo-op necessity?"

I move my head side to side in contemplation. "Solid point. I'll figure it out."

He nudges my shoulder with his. "There's a pumpkin farm down in Bluetop, at the Blisswood winery. We can go there one day."

We.

I'm wary of the term, as much as it warms my heart. "Maybe a good idea." We arrive at Jolly Joe's, and Nash is quick to open the door for me. "One scoop of blueberry and one scoop of rainbow sherbet per your usual? The ice cream of senior citizens."

Nash seems surprised. "You remember my ice cream flavor choice?"

"Of course, I do. How many times have we been here?"

A fond smile shades his face. "Probably too many to count, Ms. Chocolate Cherry Shake."

My mouth turns to an O shape. "Seems you remember, too. It's a classic flavor," I protest.

We find our way to a table, and I get situated as Nash prepares to order at the counter. "For the little guy?"

"I don't really let him have too much sugar, but they say the vanilla bean here has the least amount, so perhaps a small scoop of that."

"Got it."

Finding a table, I decide to leave Bo in his stroller and hand him a soft book with different activities, it should keep him occupied. My eyes drift to Nash ordering with his suave smile that he gives everyone. I hate that it's the little things that bring back memories that makes me twist inside.

"So, you watched the game?" Nash wipes a hand through his sweaty hair while he holds his helmet to the side, with the background noise of the arena. His face is red, and he still causes my middle to swirl. I was up in Michigan to visit a friend from college and Nash left tickets for us.

"Well, I'm here, aren't I?" I tease.

He's nearly bashful and glances away while he licks his lips. When his sight returns to me, I think we might be melting. It's been a few years since we both acted on a spark, because who knew a simple kiss could cause years of attraction to grow. The seldom times that we saw one another since, we left it as a magnetism between us that we never acted on. But tonight feels different.

"What are you doing after?"

"My friend and I were going to probably get a drink."

A devilish grin hits his mouth. "I need to change, but I'll text you a place where we can all meet."

I snicker a laugh. "Something feels like this isn't an innocent 'let's go for ice cream' suggestion."

That grin is my undoing. "It's really not. But I think you knew that when you came here."

"Earth to Summer." Nash waves a hand in front of my face, and it snaps me back to reality, brushing thoughts of how our secret months began.

I forcefully form a smile. "Yeah, sorry, just… remembering something for work."

Nash slides into the booth, not entirely convinced, and thanks the waitress for following with the ice cream and shake. "You have work tomorrow?" he asks me.

"Yeah. You're going to meet with your parents' realtor?" He nods in answer. "Sounds like we're busy then. Bo will be with the babysitter, so everything is on schedule."

"Cool."

I try not to look at him in a different way. It's just odd to be sitting here as if life is normal… and the three of us are together.

"I forgot to ask you how your brother is," Nash says. Yep, general everyday conversation.

"Keats is doing well. Checks up on me far too much, but hey, who doesn't?"

My brother is older than me by a few years and just moved a few towns over after living in the city. He's on the legal counsel for the Lake Spark Spinners. We're close, as our parents kind of live in their own world, divorced and now living with new spouses who don't get our approval.

Nash watches me intently with understanding. "That's good to hear."

"Your mom mentioned in the group chat that she enjoyed seeing a photo of you and Bo together."

He beams an honest smile. "Yeah, took it when you were getting ready. Figured, it would make them happy." His attention turns to Bo who is busy chewing on the corner of his book. Nash leans over to take the book away. "Come on, buddy, let's trade that for some ice cream."

Nash slides the small cup of ice cream his way and grabs the small spoon. I must be motionless as I watch everything unfold in front of me. The way he flawlessly offers Bo a small bite and then waits before scooping up another. No experience with babies my ass, he must have lied.

I have to wonder. "Did you ever want kids? I mean, with whomever you might have dated… in the past." My face flushes with uncomfortable warmth. I shouldn't be asking this.

It causes Nash to plop the spoon back into the bowl. "No bullshit, Summer. You asked that, and you're not sure why, except it's more than curiosity." His face is serious. "To answer your question. No. Why? Because there hasn't been anyone remotely close to y—" He stops short of what I'm well aware he is about to say.

My chest wants to burst, and my throat closes. He's right. I wanted to hear him say that there wasn't anyone else. Maybe I wanted him to suffer for pushing me away all those years ago or maybe I wanted him to confirm that I'm not crazy in my theories. Either way, the truth is now out in the open.

We both sit here, trying to understand what to say or do. Ease hits us when Bo squeaks a noise and steals our attention, immediately causing both of us to laugh. He managed to get his fingers into the ice cream.

"Uh-oh, we have a misfit in training." Nash slides the bowl away while I grab a napkin.

"Must run in the family." Our eyes connect in recognition.

Because Nash has always done things in his own way.

Which means he will do the same now that he's back in Lake Spark.

————

"This is pretty good," Lexi informs me with a full mouth as we sit by the turned-off fireplace in the inn's lobby.

I hold up a small wrapped candy. "I think so. I mean, we have the welcome sugar cookies now shaped in pumpkins and ghosts. Now we also have homemade Halloween candy with Dizzy Duck Inn wrappers."

"A perfect touch."

"Yeah, completely." I drop the caramel back into the bowl. Lexi swallows her candy, and the way she's studying me is unnerving. "What?" I wonder.

"Are you okay? You seem distant. Not in a bad way, just distant in a different way."

A long exhale leaves my lungs. "I don't know anymore. It's more Nash reappearing in my life."

"Hmm. Is it not going well with him following Zac's wishes?"

I press my lips together. "For Bo, it's fine. For me?" My head tips to the side. "Not so much. He's stirring up too much."

"About Zac?"

My mouth crosses from one side to the other. "No… Nash and I."

Lexi surveys the area to ensure we're all alone, and despite nobody in sight, she still scoots closer to me. "What about you two, exactly?"

"We were together once. Long before Zac."

She offers me a comforting look. "I kind of figured. You just never talked about it."

My shoulders lift to my ears. "Kind of hard to. I married his brother. But Nash coming back stirs up a pot of memories, remorse for even thinking some of things that are running through my head…" I begin to list.

She touches my arm. "If you mean Zac, well, he isn't around to judge," she delicately reminds me.

"I don't know what he can judge me for, except it feels like something. A tide is changing. I could say it was Nash and me fighting, but in truth, it moved as soon as he returned. And I don't know what to do." My lips begin to quiver because everything inside of me hurts, wants, and hopes all in one.

Lexi offers me a hug and soothes my back with her palm. "Maybe this is what you need to move on. We all mourn in different ways."

I begin to play with the ends of my hair. "Perhaps so. I'm just scared shitless that a door to the past might be reopened. I'm not sure it's the right thing to do."

I always feel appreciation when my friends listen without judgment. I've never shared the full story of the dynamics between me and the Nix brothers, but they would be blind not to see that there is something far too deep. A wound that I'm wondering if it could ever be healed.

The two wounds they caused. Or was it me?

"There isn't a timeframe for when you can move on. Or

explore what needs to be. Maybe that's what you need? Clarity, and that only can happen in a way that works for you."

My lips quirk out, and everything inside of me is one big hurricane brewing. "You're right."

"Good, because Nash just arrived with the other owners who use inn meetings as an excuse to just have a good time," she nervously states with a droll smile.

We both stand, and she heads straight to her husband. Stone walks to the reception desk to ask something, and Nash stays put. But I don't say anything; my chest visibly moving up and down is enough of a message.

"How was your meeting? Or rather time at the ice rink? I can only imagine it was all productive," Lexi teases her husband and pats his chest.

Holden circles his eyes between all of us, with the stiffness between me and Nash gnawing away at our current loss of clarity. "Not productive at all except for getting some tension out. Funny how skating and hockey pucks can do that."

She yanks his arm slightly, well aware that his observation is only multiplying the strain in here.

My only option is to escape when Nash doesn't say anything, instead he wipes his thumb across his jaw. "I'm going to leave you all. Need to check on one of the rooms. A guest had a special request before they arrive," I explain.

I dart away before anyone can say anything.

My powerwalk doesn't seem to be fast enough because when I'm upstairs pulling a key out of my pocket to unlock the door, I feel him near even if I don't see him.

"Go away, Nash," I request, although I know that it falls on deaf ears.

He steps closer. "I don't think I can. I think that you are avoiding the obvious."

I refuse to meet his gaze. "Humor me," I tell him dryly.

"The shift between us since the other day, it's changed things. Neither one of us has figured out what."

Fumbling with the key, I choose not to answer.

"Summer, it's impossible. Always has been between us. Except now it's anything but and that scares the hell out of me, which means it scares the hell out of you. Tell me I'm wrong." He reaches out to grab my arm when I get the door open.

My heart flips, my throat tightens, and a turmoil of emotion barrels up inside of me. I can't face him, I shouldn't face him.

But I do.

A mere glance and then I do it.

My hands plunge forward and grip his shoulders as I slam my lips onto his, a world of memories hitting me like a drug.

Instantly, he wraps his arm around me with pure reverence. Our lips don't need to explore, because they are meeting again in a fierce return. Hard, crushing, and tender, yet fast all the same.

We tumble into the room, our mouths not parting, instead tilting to get more. Our tongues greet one another in a reunion. I swear my body reacts as if no time has passed between Nash and me.

It's so fierce and desperate. I'm not sure who is murmuring and who is leading. The air I breathe is Nash's again. No thoughts of the time between us interfering. He kisses me just as he did when I was his.

Why aren't our mouths more hesitant? Why is my entire body easing into Nash just as a piece fits into a puzzle?

Then we slow, with his hands sliding up to cradle my face. Our lips soften, they chase, they part, they return. We stop. Our foreheads touching and our bodies still connected, I soak in this moment.

Wondering if this is the circle that leads back to a starting point.

Nash. Oh, Nash.

You came back wanting to fulfill a promise, caring for me. That was the request. I'm not sure taking my heart back was part of that.

It's simple. I want to stay. But something still inside me is enough to cause me to flee.

"Nash, this can't or can or, I don't know… just, I have to go."

I begin to escape, but he pulls me back. "Summer."

My eyes strike up to meet his that are full of devotion to his new plan. Still, I need to breathe in air that isn't drenched in Nash's presence. "Nash," I plead.

He nods subtly in understanding and quickly gives me a kiss on my forehead as a parting gift right before I leave.

Because I'm running away from the inevitable.

SUMMER

I rush through the hotel until I'm outside in the crisp autumn air. It's nearly a march that gets me to the dock. Hearing my name being called causes me to groan and look up, with my hand cradling my neck as if a gentle massage will do something in this moment.

"Summer, wait!"

Of course, Nash would follow me. How could I think that I would get off so lucky? A moment to process isn't in the books today.

"Go away, Nash," I sneer.

It only adds fuel, and Nash continues his quest to arrive right in front of me. He extends his arm to touch my elbow, but I yank my arm away with a scowl.

"I was going to give you space, but I can't. We should talk about this." He's adamant.

I scoff a laugh to myself. "I don't even know where to begin." My eyes move in all directions as I become aware of another fact. "How the hell do we keep ending up on this dock?"

Fuck him for smirking. "Maybe this time we won't end

up in the water." My death stare causes him to sober up his humor. "This was always a spot for us, long before. It seems it hasn't changed. What better location to talk than here? The guests get live entertainment, too." His attempt to make me laugh falls flat.

I charge forward and grip his shirt in pure frustration. "Now is not the time for jokes. I'm about to have a meltdown. No, *I am* melting down."

Nash remains composed and encircles my wrists to keep my arms in place. "Why is that?"

It's happening again today. That wave of an uncontrollable blur of feelings cannonballing through me. "Because I feel guilty. It's crazy, but I do. I should still be mourning, not making out with my dead husband's brother. It feels like I'm still sneaking around behind his back."

My words must hit Nash hard as he instantly recoils, letting my wrists fall. "Damn it, Summer. That thought has to snap out of your head."

I shake my head. "It confuses me."

"No shit. Your mixed thoughts caused you to kiss me."

"I wanted to see if that fire is still between us," I almost shout then realize what I just admitted and halt.

Nash snickers. "You really needed to test that? That's a bad excuse."

I grab my hair as I sink through a hole. "Is it? Back then, you let me go. You moved on as if I was a mistake. Why wouldn't I have my guard up?"

His face turns dark, his eyes seething with a mix of anger. "You want to know something, Summer?" I look blankly at him because it wasn't a question. "That necklace that you sometimes wear? The one hanging around your neck?" My eyes drop down, and I clasp the treasure chest. "I told him to get it. He was determined to buy you a flower or some shit like that, and I told him he should get you the treasure chest, a lucky guess I said. I left before I could see if he heard me or not. Seems he did. And you know why I told him?"

I swallow, wanting my heart to stop the spark that might explode. "Don't tell me," I breathlessly implore.

His eyes inform me that he won't listen to me. "Because you never fucking left my mind."

My eyes sting with tears. "You're making this worse."

He steps to me and slides his hand along my cheek to the back of my head, giving me no choice but to face his resolve. "I'm supposed to be in Lake Spark to make it better."

"Everything hurts," I simply answer.

His thumb wipes away a lone tear falling down my cheek, and he pauses for a second when his sight locks on the view of my scar. "It doesn't need to." His whisper scrapes his throat.

My cheek nestles into his palm. "I'm not sure what that looks like yet."

Nash gives me a comforting look. "Me neither, but I want to find out."

My heart is gravitating toward him. I'm conflicted about whether I should feel guilty or not.

"I need to get out of here."

The corner of his mouth lifts. "Are you sure you don't want to push me into the water?"

He always knows when to attempt to calm me. "Shut up, Nash." I'm not in the mood.

His hand falls away, and I give myself a moment to study him, wondering about his intentions now that he's back.

It's clear as day, he has no qualms about what he wants, and at least that's honest.

———

SITTING on the couch in the living room, I have music on and pour myself a glass of wine then set the bottle on the coffee table. Bo is asleep, and I'm aware that Nash will be returning home any moment. I'm sure he found every excuse under the sun to stay away for the last few hours. My small sip turns into a less-than-elegant near chug. It's been that kind of day.

The key turning in the lock immediately heightens my blood pressure because it's Nash returning. Clearing my head only brought me a tiny ounce of transparency. If there weren't the factor of being a widow, then without a doubt I would explore the magnetic friction that Nash and I have.

If I look back through the years, I shouldn't have been so blind. We had a loosened knot that only needed to be retightened. Loyalty was in the way, and now there is a ghost between us, and this dynamic is new to me.

I glance up when I hear the door close, and Nash slowly walks my way with hesitation, yet his piercing eyes are still far too powerful.

"I was wondering if I needed to send out a search dog or something." I smile nervously.

"Nah, just wanted to give you space and figured you would be in good company with a bottle of white." He indicates with his head to the bottle on the living room table.

"Seemed only fitting. Want a glass?"

"I'll grab a beer." He disappears into the kitchen, and after the sound of the fridge closing, I hear the snap of the bottle cap. Nash is quick to return with a bottle, and he swaggers his way to the couch to sit down on the opposite end of the sofa, a solid no-man's land between us.

I thrum my fingers on my thigh. "Uhm, you can put on the sports channel or something. I know pre-season games are over and the season is starting."

He smiles to himself. "Very honorable of you, but I

wanted to ask… is it better if I stay at the Dizzy Duck? I know my brother wanted me to stay here to ensure you're okay, but I might be making this worse for you."

"No," I raise my voice, then calm. "I mean, it's fine. I don't want you to go. It's good for Bo, and I'm not sure…" I avoid meeting his eyes, and I stare at my bare ring finger. "I don't think staying at the Dizzy Duck would matter. You're still in Lake Spark. Still close enough to do damage."

"Damage. Great." His tone is edged.

My hand rockets up to relax his thoughts, and I scooch over on the couch to bring up my legs and bare feet to cross and half face him. "No, I mean… It's just, I would still be a hot mess of feelings, so might as well get a baby-oatmeal maker out of the deal."

Relief hits him. "Okay then."

"As… well, as long as it's okay for you. It's not just me having issues here, right?"

His jaw juts out as if he's wondering where I'm going with this. "Is that so?" He's messing with me. Or is he? "Maybe when I first got back, but it's becoming too obvious what to do. I can handle that… I've accepted that."

He slides over a little, and our space is closing even more. Heat rises under my skin, and my face must appear flushed. "Summer, I'm not going to feel guilty. I've come to the conclusion that maybe my way of mourning is to be near you. To be *with* you."

My eyes dip low, and I see my charm necklace hanging and floating in the air, and I use it to divert us. "It seems the Nix brothers have a thing for giving me jewelry. A ring and a necklace." Because it was really Nash, wasn't it?

"I'm angry he was the one who gave the necklace to you, if that's any consolation."

My skin burns from the contrast of thoughts due to that admission. "You shouldn't say things like that."

Because I might agree.

Our eyes linger again, the air nearly suffocating. Nash's finger bolts out and hooks under my chin to draw my attention to him, with his fortitude written all over his face. "There's something I've wanted to do since I've been back."

The room is beginning to spin as every ounce of anticipation inside me surges, and I attempt to keep it down. "I don't think I want to know," I rasp.

Nash leans in. "And I don't care."

My chest panics that he is going to try and kiss me, but his lips bypass my mouth and do something much worse. They brush along the scar above my eyebrow. My entire body melts when Nash gently kisses it.

"I'm sorry," he murmurs against my skin.

I'm not sure how to breathe anymore, as the room seems to be fading around us. "Nash."

"I did this to you… and I'm the selfish guy who not only thinks you're beautiful but who is slightly satisfied that every day you are reminded of me."

As twisted as it sounds, the possessiveness that he has ignites something inside of me. His hands stay firmly planted to hold my head when he withdraws slightly.

"Every time I look in the mirror, there is no escape from you," I confess in a whisper.

He follows the path of his fingers as he lifts a part of my hair, then he places it behind my shoulder. "You're allowed to let your walls down if that's what you need."

Every part of my body is reacting. From my head to my toes and all parts in between, including my sensitive area that longs to be touched.

"Tell me to get up and leave," I plead, with my throat feeling dry.

His mouth quirks out, and Nash's eyes remain persistent with his beliefs. "I'm selfish, remember? You were mine first, so you know I won't tell you to run."

I nod gently, aware that the inevitable is happening.

Slowly we both lean in to let our lips meet. It's a softer kiss than earlier today, sensual and longing spilling out. I hate as much as I love how our mouths perfectly fit.

Our tongues delve in with their tips gently tickling each other, making me want more. Nash cradles my head between his hands to kiss me deeper, to hold onto me so I won't fall. In truth, I already did within.

A murmur fills my throat, and I grip his arms, wanting to ensure that I stay completely in place because I don't want to escape this time. Our mouths part only to find one another again, this time more fervent and insistent. We are past going slow.

I feel my body naturally lead and guide Nash to sit back, and I adjust my legs until I'm straddling him, with our mouths still intact for a kiss, except his hands drop to my waist, his fingers sneaking under the fabric of my tank top. He slowly drags my shirt up, and I want more, too. My hands search between us for his shirt, and I begin to tug as I want it gone. He abandons me for a second to whip his shirt up and off. Meanwhile, I finish the job of getting my own shirt off, leaving me in a bra.

My head falls back as Nash's mouth brushes down my throat to my collarbone that he kisses gently. I place the palms of my hands against his bare chest to create a little space. I check in that we're really going to do this. It appears that all our fears have vanished. With urgency, we return to our exploration of one another. Nash's lips graze my cleavage while his fingers work the clasp behind me. Instantly, my breasts peek out, and his mouth begins to tease my nipple. Everything in me is painfully throbbing for his touch.

Dampness from my pussy seeps through my yoga pants, and I swirl my hips against him. Nash always liked to lead and could read my body, always giving me what I needed. It seems now is no different. He guides me back until my head lands on a cushion, and he hovers over me while we kiss.

But my lips feel vacant when he sits up on his knees to pull my yoga pants down while I raise my legs. His eyes are on me, hungry.

"My beautiful Summer," he whispers. The pants find a home on the floor, and his wicked eyes warn me as his mouth coasts up my legs, slowing on my thighs for a few soft kisses and giving me agony in anticipation.

"Nash."

He teases my thighs with his lips, drawing lazy patterns. His fingers slide up and rub against my panties. I'm not ashamed how soaked I am for him, and he's pleased as he moans in response. Slipping under the fabric to glide along my pussy, he finds my clit, and my entire body tilts up in response. Nash's palm splays against my stomach to calm me, and I'm rewarded with his mouth kissing me over the fabric on that sensitive spot.

"Don't stop." I breathe out my torture.

He pauses for a second. "I never wanted to." Then he returns to worshipping me.

Except his sentence had more meaning. He never wanted to leave and stop us all those years ago… but loyalty got in the way.

My eyes close, taking in the overflow of desire, feeling my panties disappear, and the sound of Nash's zipper filling my ears.

"Tell me I can take you like this." It's not a question, more of a plea.

I lick my lips. "I have an IUD. And I know you would never…" It doesn't matter about logistics now. He would never hurt me physically.

"I want to get lost in you again," he mutters as he parts my thighs open and kisses me by my knee.

I'm already lost in him, this, everything.

The moment he enters me with just his tip, we both moan together. It's been too long, and our tension incinerates as he pumps deeper until I'm full and stretched. Every move causing tremors through my body.

"Summer." His warm breath tickles me, and his mouth caresses my breast as he gently thrusts inside me.

My nails scrape his back to bring him deeper. It sets him off, and our pace changes to a hurried need to let go together. With our eyes connected, it's intense as our bodies become one with him inside me, which is why we let go.

I've needed him.

It's all clear to me now.

I've missed him. That I already knew.

When we settle into an embrace in our afterglow, with Nash tossing a blanket from the back of the sofa over us and my head resting firmly against his chest, there is another thought that hits me.

I was supposed to end up back in his arms.

But why does my heart twist so much?

My fingers trail along Summer's arm as we lie on the couch with a throw blanket loosely draped over her. All the more reason why I need to keep her naked body warm and close to me.

"This has to be our last time," she whispers weakly as her eyes follow her fingertips tracing my chest.

"Then why are you still in my arms?"

"Maybe I want to get every moment I can," she answers.

I inhale the scent of her hair, a familiar calmness coming over me. "I'm surprised you haven't run away yet. But here you stay." Her lips brush along my chest, and she settles again with her cheek resting against my body as I begin to stroke her hair.

"It's hard to… It feels like we are picking up from the last moment I was in your arms like this. Except there's time between us, and I'm not sure if it haunts me or not."

"Let go, Summer. Speak without thought. Otherwise, you'll be miserable."

"I don't like being alone," she laments.

I squeeze her tighter. "You're not. You don't need to fight it. I'm not going to run away."

"You did last time."

My body stills for a second due to the reminder. "Things change. Life changed."

She gave a gift to my brother. My nephew is in the picture. The challenges seem vague in the future for us, but that's better than nothing.

Our fingers gravitate toward one another and intertwine to move our hands together. "It feels like we've come full circle if I'm honest. It was you, then not, and now I'm back to you. The hole in my heart for many reasons is beginning to diminish slightly, barely."

"That's a start."

We lie here in silence in an embrace that is more than comfort; it's right.

"I remember you and I being like this for hours. Nobody knew. Now it seems to be a repeat, except I haven't figured out if the stakes are higher."

Inside of me there is a fight to shake her and tell her it's all going to be okay. In truth, this is a whole new realm for all of us. Both Summer and I want to honor Zac and the time since he has passed. Except for me, my timer is up. Does that make me a bad person?

Am I just swooping in because I have my chance to have Summer again? We haven't even figured out if my brother is the ghost that will haunt us or guide us. I'm just choosing the latter.

"Remember when you and I would order in food so we would never be apart? Just you and me barely clothed and talking?" she asks.

"I wouldn't forget something like that." We would lie in bed for hours, and I would take her too many times to count.

"We were in our own world. That's what I want now." Summer lifts her head to bring her gaze to mine. "I need to process what's happening between you and me. Is this what consolation is, or do people get a second chance in the saddest of circumstances?"

What she says is wise. We could both be blinded by lust, even if I'm confident that I won't let go this time.

"I'll give us that," I agree.

Her sigh for once sounds comforting. Summer's letting go, even if just for tonight.

"I should probably go to sleep. I need to be at the Dizzy Duck early," she mentions yet doesn't make an effort to move.

Nor do I encourage her to leave our island on the couch. My eyes roam the room, purposely avoiding any photos on mantels, and I'm relieved that the box of blocks is an easy distraction. "Summer."

"Mmhmm." She sounds drowsy.

"I'm sorry I didn't show up when Bo was born."

I wasn't a man. I couldn't put my pride to the side, instead wallowing in what I didn't have.

Summer adjusts her body again, and her fingers grip my jaw to guide my gaze to hers. "It's okay. You showed up eventually."

She isn't mad at me now, but I know she was, and maybe now it's just washed away.

Something has been stirring in me lately, and I should tell her. "I'm not here because I feel like I owe it to someone to be here for Bo. I *want* to be here for him."

Her mouth shifts to a faint smile. "It seems you just went from a five to a six on the baby scale."

"I need to work on my diaper changing, is that it? Is that why I'm not excelling at a faster rate to a ten?"

She chuckles faintly. "Probably. Now I think I need to leave this sofa purely because my side is beginning to ache. I'm impressed that we both fit here like this."

"We're kind of one body right now." And it's the only fit that will be the right size.

"True. Still, my hip is going to hate me tomorrow."

That's reasonable, which is why I shuffle with her to sitting up with the blanket carelessly covering her breasts. We both take a moment to stretch before Summer stands and gazes at me peculiarly. "Do you think you can sleep with me?"

My eyes grow big. "I was supposed to return to my room?" I'm teasing her because it probably was an option in her head.

"I shouldn't answer that," she admits right before she peers up with her eyes vulnerable. "I don't want to sleep alone. Not tonight."

"Then I'll follow you."

Her eyes gleam with appreciation.

I grab my boxer briefs and tell her to go on ahead. Picking up the beer bottle and wine glass, I bring them to the kitchen counter and will worry about them tomorrow. When I'm upstairs, I do a quick check through the door that's ajar to Bo's room, and I hear white noise and see the glow of the blue nightlight that projects stars. It's cute. I head to my room, grab a shirt, and check myself in the bathroom. Settling in for the night sounds good right now.

Arriving at Summer's room, I remember she mentioned the timeline of moving into the house which already erased one equation of this whole situation. Summer is on her side under the covers, now in a cotton t-shirt.

"Hey," she greets me shyly.

I saunter to the bed and then slide under the blankets to

join her. We face one another and lie on our sides. "You're still warm," she grins.

"Uh, should I be ice?" I wonder.

"No, it's just I remember sleeping with you and you radiated so much body heat that you had no choice but to take your shirt off."

My tongue runs along my bottom lip. "It will probably happen again, if that's okay?"

Her hands rest under her cheek and her smile feels earnest. "It is. So just hold me," she requests.

I scoop Summer close, encasing my body to hers. "You never need to ask."

"Then maybe I never asked enough," she states softly.

Quieting her, I seal her lips with a tender kiss, refusing to recall why she couldn't ask.

———

OF COURSE, I woke to a cold bed because Summer slipped out without detection this morning. I'm not surprised, but that doesn't mean I'm not going to confront it.

Which is exactly why I'm leaning against the front desk in the Dizzy Duck with my ankles crossed and snacking on a pumpkin-shaped sugar cookie, thankful that I didn't get the ghost-shaped one because that would be too fucking relevant.

"I don't know, I'm kind of thinking that the whole traditional Christmas gala has to return. It's stuffy, and my parents loved it. It was kind of a competition with the Lake Spark Country Club, but the Dizzy Duck Inn had a bit more holiday festivity. You know? Like, a resemblance to the setting of that game Clue but with a holiday theme," I explain to Stuart behind the front desk.

He listens with interest. "You mean, like a murder mystery kind of night?"

I snap my fingers. "Ooh, that's a good thought. I think that historical museum over in Everhope does one of those. We need one a bit closer, and it seems that we have a place. I should run that by Holden and Stone." I roll my shoulders back with a cocky tone. "I should have given this place more attention the last few years. I'm full of great ideas."

"Hey, Stuart, do you know when the coffee repair guy is coming? That machine Holden ordered way back keeps breaking down. It's becoming a nuisance," Summer asks as she focuses on a few papers in her hand.

"Kind of like me?"

Her eyes shoot up. "Shit," she mutters to herself, clearly being caught out and aware this was going to happen.

I give Stuart a warning glare to disappear, and he gets the message.

"Avoiding me is classic," I inform her.

She rolls her eyes. "Can we just leave it?"

Approaching her, I tsk my tongue. "No. So either we talk here or I'm happy to carry you to the dock since you tend not to shut up there."

Summer seems irritated. "Nash, now isn't the time—"

I shove my half-eaten cookie into her mouth and her sound is muffled. "I need you quiet."

She wipes the back of her hand across her mouth as she chews and swallows the cookie. "What the hell, Nash," she barks.

"You're freaking out, I know you are."

"This is happening so fast. You're back a week and I'm sharing a bed with you. I should feel guilty or… it's only been a few months since…" She is quick to scan the room and sees we are alone. "A few months as a widow. Am I dishonoring him by ending up in bed with you? I don't know the timeline for these things."

"There isn't one," I blankly remind her.

Summer jabs a finger into my chest. "Why aren't you feeling the same way? This must be a slap in Zac's face. Don't you feel guilty?"

"No." I'm direct. My bluntness causes her eyes to spear me with surprise, as she wasn't expecting me to say that. "Not today, at least." Which makes me an asshole, I'm sure.

She blinks as she tries to contemplate my answer. It's a long silence. Idling in some ways, too.

The tip of her tongue darts out to lick a crumb away. "Damn, the seasonal cookies are good." She shakes her head, realizing she's slightly off track. "Nash, I'm…" She heaves a breath and straightens her posture. "It just feels…"

I cross my arms. "I'm waiting, otherwise that dock is calling our name, and throwing you over my shoulder is no issue for me."

Summer provides me with a pointed look. "Fine. My sentence as a non-flustered human is that this thing between us, it just feels… gravitating, impossible to ignore. But a fucking clock is taunting me; I should be taking longer to mourn."

"Language, Summer," I goad her to try and get the faintest of smiles from her. But then I step closer, realizing the magnitude of her thoughts. "Don't run away. We'll figure it out together. I'm also on the same timeline of history as you."

"Everyone doesn't stare at you the same way," she hisses softly. It kills me that she appears to fear shame.

"Summer, who cares what people think? You have a backbone. Don't let anyone but me get to you."

She exhales a deep breath as she soaks in my words. "Okay."

I touch her shoulder delicately. "Okay, you're saying it to get rid of me now, or okay because you are agreeing?"

She's exhausted by me, but her smile developing means she doesn't mind. "Okay, I am agreeing." She still sounds a bit stubborn, and I'm still not 100% convinced.

"Can I also hold you while you sleep again tonight? Maybe tomorrow too?"

Her tongue darts to the corner of her mouth, and she contemplates for a second. "Well... considering last night, then it would feel kind of... empty sleeping alone. So, yes."

I grin at her response, as it is the only answer for me.

Her hand shoos me away. "Now go. I need to get back to work, so can you just..." She ushers me in the direction where I need to go, but I don't budge.

I have to throw in my smug card. "I partly own this place. I'm sure I can ensure you don't get in trouble if you want to grab lunch as two people trying to figure out life together."

Summer looks away, but her light demeanor remains. "Not today. I really do want to work to ensure I finish on time to let the babysitter go."

"Want me to do that? Rumor has it if I add pick-up duty to my roster, then I might move up from a six to a seven on the baby scale."

Summer chuckles. "Get out of here. And no, I'll do it."

All the complications between us seem to fade away for these few moments. "Hey, Summer, I was..." My thumb draws a line from my mouth to my stubbled chin as I hesitate to ask, but I take the plunge anyhow. "Maybe we can do that pumpkin patch thing this weekend. It would be good to get out of Lake Spark for a day. Just you, Bo, and me."

"That could be..." She stops herself from protesting.

But another issue dawns on me. "You, uhm… you're not afraid to get in a car with me, are you?" Last time she ended up in the hospital.

She glances away then back. "No, Nash. I'm not. The accident was literally that."

"We had been arguing before," I remind her.

"Yeah, because you ended things." That's a cold splash of water, but then her entire face softens. "Everything happens for a reason, even if we don't want it that way."

I swallow, accepting her answer, even if I'm not entirely free of my guilt. "I just wanted to check. I mean, I would understand if you are."

Summer's eyes grow into large circles, clearly now humorously annoyed. "Can we close this topic? You had an idea for this weekend."

I relax a little. "Yeah, a getaway."

"A good idea. For all of us, the three of us." Summer nods and leaves me be.

The three of us. She didn't mean anything by it. Just a simple answer.

But it tugs somewhere inside of me.

Stepping into someone's shoes. Or getting a renewed chance.

Fuck.

I'm going to throw every ghost cookie, no matter how perfectly delicious, into the garbage. I have enough reminders as it is.

●13

SUMMER

Change.

That's what the fall season is a sign of.

My head rests on the back of the seat while Nash drives his SUV. I have to smile to myself because I doubt he intended for this car to become one with a sleeping baby in the back. I'm really not sure why he is sliding into the whole uncle role so easily, but he is.

Nash glances in the rearview mirror. "That kid is like a mystical baby creature or something. He's never really fussy, is he?"

I scoff a laugh. "He is. When he was born, the first month was hell. Didn't really want to sleep. Now looking back, I'm kind of grateful that he didn't. It meant Zac had more waking moments with Bo."

Way to go, Summer. Just cut the air in half again.

"I'm sorry I keep bringing up your brother." I observe Nash who stays focused on the road.

"It's okay. You don't need to be closed off about it. He is ultimately Bo's father."

I hum a sound in agreement. "That I know you support. I just don't want us to be reminded of the conflict inside of us."

"Really, it's fine. Besides, if I'm honest, it has crossed my mind today. He would have loved to have done this with Bo. Now I'm stepping in and it isn't quite the same." Nash's voice when he goes soft and exposed is more than a comfort; it lifts light inside of me as we share an understanding.

I extend my fingers to touch his arm gently. "I think we've gotten this out of the way, so let's focus on having a good day. I know the Blisswood farm is more than a winery, but someone mentioned they have a great pumpkin season with cider, too."

"It is. Their connection to Lake Spark also scores bonus points for choosing this place to visit. Sometimes, you see the brothers making a delivery in Lake Spark. They also have family there, too, as someone married Hudson Arrows's son."

"Everyone knows who is who in town." I check once more to see Bo beginning to stir. "Uh-oh, the Little Baby Creature Thing as you sometimes call him is awakening." I find it adorable the way Nash was at first unsure of being around kids, but then he glides right into being a pro at it, and I know that's going to happen today.

"Is he going to be cranky until he gets a snack?"

I nod a few times and reach for my bag on the floor by my feet to search for a soft baby cookie. "Most definitely. That's why I always come prepared." I hold up the cookie with pride, and that half-smile of his stays permanent.

"We're almost there. Like do we need one classic pumpkin or are you going to take it a notch up and we buy a few?"

"I guess as many as your arms can handle."

He chuckles. "Fair play."

Bo gives me a few blinks before he yawns, and then a smile begins to curve on his chubby little cheeks.

"Remind me to get him a Halloween costume. The Dizzy Duck has a staff party coming up, which I'm sure you know since your executive meetings are at the ice rink and very informative where lots of work gets done." I flash my eyes at him before I stretch my body to the back and hand Bo his snack.

"Whoa, whoa, whoa. It's team building, and we do discuss the Dizzy Duck."

I doubt this tremendously. "Really?"

Nash tips his head to the side and grins to himself. "Okay, we mostly listen to Holden complain about the expensive coffee machine breaking and how we are currently using a French press for coffee."

I interrupt and point my finger at him. "Which the guests actually love and feel it's a classic touch."

"Tell that to Holden. But really, the Dizzy Duck is successful without me. There isn't much to discuss."

I'm not sure how I've been so ignorant to the fact that Nash is only supposed to be in town for a short time. Suddenly, a small dose of fear swims inside of me.

Luckily broken by the car coming to a halt in the parking lot.

"Here we are. I get the stroller out of the trunk, right?" Nash asks, oblivious to my thoughts.

I unbuckle my seatbelt. "It's probably better if I use the baby carrier."

"Cool. I'll get him out before he can cause any more crumb damage to my car."

That is such a Nash thing to say, and it does the trick, as all negative thoughts fade away.

We get everything settled and Bo strapped to the front of

my body. The weather is great today, with sun and temperatures in the high 50s, but it feels warmer. The farm is gorgeous, well taken care of, and I understand why it's often a weekend hotspot.

"I know the wine is good, but since they do have two rooms for their bed-and-breakfast, then we should be wondering if we're cheating on your business investment and my place of employment," I tease.

"We're good," he assures me and zips up his jacket then yanks my arm, carefully since Bo is in his carrier. "Come on, we have a hay maze to conquer."

I laugh because it's so silly but also perfect. "I like that idea. If you get us lost, then you have to do dishes for a week."

"I'm being sentenced to a chore chart again?" This is the banter I need.

When we enter the maze, I'm already completely lost, and we haven't even turned a corner. "Remember in high school we would all head to the haunted hayride at Pioneer Park outside of town? It's like the only time of year that they don't cater to the kid population."

"That ride was scary shit. After, there was always some crazy party at someone's house that would get out of hand," Nash recalls as he debates which way we go at the fork in the road.

I playfully slap his arm. "You always went as the same thing. No costume at all."

He throws me a cocky look. "Because I didn't need to dress up. I would wear my jersey and I was set."

"Just like reality. I guess fake blood on your jersey wouldn't really be different to your hockey games."

Nash twirls his finger in the air. "Let's backtrack for a

second. You were a cat in fishnets with a skirt way too fucking short for my liking."

I cover Bo's ears and smile humorously. "Watch the language around this little guy… and I'm surprised you remember."

He looks at me as if I'm crazy. "I'm not sure any guy that night forgot."

I grin proudly to myself as we continue our stroll and approach a scarecrow. "I'm going to have to find a mom-appropriate costume for my son's first Halloween."

Nash snickers. "You rock the hot-mom thing, wear what you want."

Who would have thought our playful comments wouldn't spook me today. It feels normal, way too quickly. Leading us down a path, I feel him follow in tow.

"I can take that sentence in so many different ways." I'm having a good time, and we're flirting, too. "Priority is figuring out a costume for this little guy." I bounce Bo as his hands reach out.

"I'll do it. Let me be in charge of costume duty… for him, I mean."

My lips quirk out as I mull it over. "It should be a big thing for me to choose, but in all honesty, I don't have the brain power right now, and I'm curious what on earth you might come up with."

"Great."

We arrive at the end of the maze to face the pumpkin patch, and we both breathe in relief. "Oh, thank you, pumpkin lords. Hay is exciting for only like a minute," I pretend to speak to a higher power.

Nash nudges my shoulder with his. "Nah, you loved it. You could walk aimlessly around."

I stand taller and think about it. He's right, I'm kind of

relaxed and not overthinking for a few moments. "You have a point," I confirm. "Now pumpkins. What are you benching these days that they used to pay you millions for?"

He smirks at me and my humor. "Summer, we could easily pack the trunk full, but I'm going to say that five feels like a good number for your doorstep."

"I agree," I say and begin to unbuckle the carrier to take Bo out. I turn him around and lean down so he can touch a pumpkin, and that immediately makes me smile. In the corner of my eye, I notice that Nash is admiring the view and takes a photo with his phone. "How could I forget that we need photos?"

"Don't worry. Your superhero is here. Now come on, both of you pose." I listen to my command and face the camera, doing my best to get Bo to cooperate.

This is what we do for what feels like hours but is probably only twenty minutes. "I think we've studied the field enough and are ready to make our choices," I announce.

Nash looks at me, impressed. "Didn't realize we were doing a draft pick for pumpkins. Let's make sure they sign their entry-level contract before they reach my car."

That causes me to laugh hard, nearly making my stomach hurt, and when my laugh calms, I have to ask. "Missing the hockey life already?"

He seems to ponder it as he moves a pumpkin out of the way. "I do, actually, but my focus was getting lost anyhow."

"You had a lot going on in life, it's understandable," I sympathize.

"Maybe, or maybe I was just losing heart in the game. I don't think I miss the social life outside the rink, either."

I consider what might be going through his mind. "Then what awaits you?"

"When I arrived in Lake Spark I didn't know. Now? I'm

beginning to wonder if my brother is giving me hints to what exactly life will be."

My eyes snap to the ground to avoid our eyes meeting. "Right. Six weeks and then…"

Nash steps forward and lifts Bo from my arms, and Bo coos. "Actually, I kind of forgot that timeline. I'm too stuck on what's going on between us and how it's kind of… healing, helping, I'm not sure. Seems to be my way of coping, too."

Immediately, my sight zaps to look up, and Nash's face is stoic, but it's because he knows he's delivered a new fact to me. "I kind of thought…"

"That I would sleep with you, try to be an uncle, and leave?"

My eyes drift down, nearly ashamed of the thought. "It was the plan. Not the sleeping-together part but the request from Zac part to stay only six weeks."

"Maybe plans change. It's hard to think past tomorrow. I arrived in Lake Spark not at all thrilled with his wish, because you and I were not on the radar, and I didn't know how to process. We both were not thrilled and showed it. Now? It seems you and I are a lot more than two people dreading a request. I feel too compelled to explore this, but we can both acknowledge that we have two very different approaches of how to handle this situation."

Stepping closer to them, I feel a whoosh travel down my body. "I think I needed that clarification. The timeline factor."

A firm line forms on Nash's mouth, and he focuses his attention on Bo. "One day at a time, right, buddy?"

A second or two then I switch our focus. "Get in position," I tell him, and my hand slips into the pocket of the carrier still loosely buckled around me to grab my cell. "We need some photos of you two. Your parents will lose their cool if they see this. The number of heart emojis your parents send with every Bo picture has made me wonder if they know how to use any other emoji or just insist on pressing the same one a million times." I crack a smile because it's so true and also sweet.

"Geez, they still do that stuff? When I was playing hockey, after every game they would send me the emoji of a flexed muscle and a hockey stick, then repeat that pattern about a thousand times in one message. So don't worry, they have two more emojis in their portfolio." Nash has a warm smile glued to his face as he kneels down and holds Bo on his knee as my son reaches out for a pumpkin.

"It's not every day a parent can say they have a professional hockey player and a doctor as sons. I'm sure they were starstruck even with their own kids. Now stop stalling and give me a photo that is holiday-card worthy."

Nash ruefully shakes his head and glances down at Bo, and that's the shot. I need no more. There is love there. Bo is calm, and Nash seems invested. It's all apparent through the camera and also to me.

It's an overbearing wave of consolation.

I snap a few more photos just in case, until a hand on my shoulder causes me to bring my attention to an older woman who seems to be the grandmother of the little girl running up ahead.

"Do you want me to take a photo of you three together?" she offers.

"That's kind of you to ask. Sure." I show her the button on my screen and scurry to Bo and Nash. Leaning down and balancing on my toes, I touch Nash's shoulder for support. My other hand grabs my son's little hand, and I guess we are all smiling when the old lady takes a photo. I can't see because we all face the same direction, but I feel our elated faces.

I smile and walk back to the older woman. "Thank you so much."

"No problem. It will be a lovely picture, you're a cute little family," she compliments.

I pause for a second and soak in her words. "Thanks."

I glance over my shoulder back to Nash who is throwing goofy faces at Bo who in return is grabbing his nose. Reminding myself that it's okay to have a day to feel like myself again and be hopeful, I throw on a smile, take a deep breath, and place my cell back into the pocket.

"I think we need to load the pumpkins and grab some cider, maybe a few bottles of wine, and while we're at it, I think I saw lemon bars somewhere," I list.

"Someone just got bossy." Nash winks at me.

"That's normally your department." I clearly forgot to filter out innuendo, and now Nash has a devilish grin. My face warms, and I'm well aware that I'm blushing. "Let's just find cider, okay?" Move us along. That's my plan.

We managed to get more photos when we saw a swing by the pond and had a delicious lunch, too. The Blisswood farm doesn't really have many animals, but they let us see the horse when they discovered we're from Lake Spark, and Bo looked at the horse with wonder.

I don't think Bo will sleep on the way back to Lake Spark, but that's okay. Nash and I take a moment to rest before we start the drive, and I take this as an opportunity to catch his fingers and entwine them with mine.

"Thank you for today. It's been a while since I've gotten to kind of turn off," I admit.

Nash brings my knuckle up to his lips for a kiss that is near saccharine. "You need to go easy, Summer. You're allowed to take time when you need it. Beyond the circumstances, I can only imagine just being a mom is tough work. Guys that I used to play with looked like hell when they had a baby at home. I mean, a few even had to sleep in separate rooms away from their kids just to get proper sleep before a game. You're doing it all alone."

"I'm going to give myself a little more compassion, but distraction is also my thing."

I elongate my body and bring my hand to touch the side of his head as I kiss his lips. We're not in public in Lake Spark, nobody can judge me for being in my own little world with Nash. He returns the kiss in full, and it causes me to murmur because it's so perfectly tender, and I wanted it like this, which is why I initiated our lips finding one another. My thumb rubs a circle on his gruff cheek when I pull away with our foreheads touching.

"I've missed this. Being with you as if the world can stop. Kissing you when I want," I convey to him.

"Me too, Summer. Me too." He kisses the tip of my nose.

A break of a cry begins, only to build.

"You totally jinxed us earlier by saying he never cries." I pull away with a wide grin.

Nash chuckles as he starts the car, and I reach back to set the pacifier back in Bo's mouth.

Today felt like a family day, and that's always good for the soul.

WITH MY LONG T-SHIRT ON, I flop onto the bed where Nash is waiting. It's nice having someone in bed, ready to welcome you with open arms. It's been a very long time since I've had this with a strong flame underneath. My marriage was cuddly, but it lacked the fire. But now Nash is here, and he always had the match.

Straddling him, he grips my hips as he sits up. "You're too beautiful," he murmurs when his lips lightly press into the curve of my neck.

"You've mentioned once or twice, Mr. Ages Well."

Nash growls where my throat meets my collarbone. "Stroking my ego when we're in bed together is a very risky move."

My forearms come up to rest on his shoulders, with my hands linking behind his neck. My pussy is right on top of his hard shaft, and this sheet around his waist has to go or it will just end up a tangled mess.

"I remember all of your risky moves, Nash." My voice is sultry, and I'm so turned on in this moment that I'm about to beg.

Our eyes check in with one another, a mirror of simmering determination. "We both seem to remember." It's a scraped whisper from his throat.

Something inside of me is about to explode, and it's a battle between my pussy and my chest. It's only made worse when he tosses me off and ensures I land on my back, with his body floating over me.

"Arms above your head, Summer." His eyes are piercing me and his voice sweltering. Here is demanding Nash. The Nash that is a reminder that his steely exterior sometimes transfers over into the bedroom.

I obey without question, and I'm rewarded with his hand skimming up my thigh. "I appreciate that you came to bed with no panties. It gets us to our destination sooner."

My entire body curves up into him to build friction. "Where might that be?" I coo.

"My mouth on your pussy right before my cock fills you up."

A moan escapes me from the pure thought. "You're wasting time it seems by talking right now."

That causes him to dare me to taunt him again. "I have no problem flipping you to your stomach to take you right away."

My knees butterfly out, offering myself to him, and the moment his fingers touch my pussy, I'm desperate for him.

Passion is our thing. It's why we could barely be in a room together for years. Patience seems to have paid off, and I ignore every thought of why that is.

Because today I got to see that now can be better if I take steps to move on.

● **14**

NASH

I'm kissing her again.

We're in the same bed again.

And the way Summer's cheeks are tight, with her swollen lips gently pulled up, it seems she can experience a moment when she is less numb again.

Summer's eyes draw down to me as my mouth trails below her belly while my splayed hands push the thin fabric of her shirt up until my palm rests between her breasts. My mouth? There is only one direction where I plan to go, and she eases me down by weaving her fingers through my hair.

My lips pause and I peer up. "Arms, Summer," I prompt her again.

A sound escapes her mouth to make me aware that she's toying with me. She knew I would remind her of what I want. She ceremoniously stretches her arms over her head again, and I continue my journey, landing right where I want.

My tongue flicks out to sweep across her clit, and we both marvel in the instant electricity that intensifies between us. Her taste on my tongue makes me eager for more, and my dick is ready to plunge inside of her.

Hooking my arms underneath her knees, I widen her and dive in again to lap her up and down a few times until I circle her clit again then suck. Her body jolts from the sensation, and pride roars through me that her body is mine to play with.

"I'm addicted to you all over," I murmur to her and scrape my lips along her inner thigh, with her silky skin imprinting on my lips.

"Nash, I need you," she purrs as she props her upper body up on her elbows, enabling her to receive a better view of me.

My eyes feel stormy. Summer is mine, only mine, and I'm scared I might reach so deep inside of her that she will scream, but today was a special day. Or at least, it felt that way. A glimpse of what I once dreamed then let go of when she was no longer mine, and apparently, I didn't need to let go, only hold on and wait.

I drop her legs because my body now provides the stability to keep her open since I'm quick to drift over Summer to steal a kiss, a quick one that I receive before her hand comes up to caress my cheek. Our eyes seal together, with nothing from the outside world able to break this moment.

Between us, our hands meet to pull down my boxer briefs, and she wraps her hand around my length, causing my eyes to close for a few seconds to enjoy Summer having me in her hold.

"Please, Nash," she begs, already guiding my shaft to where she needs me.

"Summer, I warned you. Hands above your head. Your body is mine, and I'll ensure we both get what we need." My fingers lock around her wrists to rocket her arms straight back up to where they need to stay. Her fraught body displays her perfectly round breasts with tight hard nipples, and naturally, I need to tease her with my fingers and tongue. A tug and a twist, and her hips rise as she attempts to get me inside of her.

"The moment I'm inside of you, we need to keep you quiet. I'm not going to go slow or easy. I'm going to take and take until you're filled with me, understand?" I caution her.

She nods up and down once with a sly grin.

I sit up on my knees to yank her hips closer to me, and as soon as I find my position, I enter Summer's snug fit and follow her body up until she's underneath me. Slamming into her, both our bodies quiver from the force. I pump into her a few times, and Summer wraps her legs around me, using me to hang on. Maybe I should worry more about hurting her, but our eyes confirm that like this is for us. We have years to make up for. It was the fucking longest full circle of my life, and with every thrust into Summer, I let her body know that it's mine now. Only mine, and I have no plans to let that go.

My mouth covers hers as her moan can no longer be kept quiet, with the mattress moving when I take over her body fully. Maybe she'll ache tomorrow, but as long as she doesn't tell me to stop, I'm going to ensure she's aware that I have a claim on her.

We move in rhythm, and as my speed quickens, she uses my shoulder to muffle her sounds as I grunt. Her teeth sink into my skin in a playful manner, but it keeps every part of Summer connected to me.

Even when we start to shake together, we both stay as one.

I like that she doesn't go straight to the bathroom to clean up. I'm still inside of her, and it feels territorial.

"Is this us making up for lost time? Or just eager to fuck one another's brains out," I wonder as my breath begins to cool off. Gravity takes over, causing me to slip out of her and land on my back next to her.

Summer rolls to her side to give me an amused glance and pats my chest. "Nah, you've never really done fragile or treated me like I was once a virgin, so don't you worry, you're sticking to tradition."

She's funny, this one. "Okay, in that case, you'll be waking up with me fucking you from behind."

"Such a hardship," she teases then returns to her back to look at the ceiling.

I peel the duvet up and over us. "Younger us were a little wild at times."

Summer snorts out a laugh. "You mean handcuffing me to your bed or kitchen escapades?"

"Excuse me, Miss Go Down on Me in the Shower, even when I was running late for practice."

"Well, it was fun. Besides, I'm happy you have the memories, because windows of opportunities are not in our favor with a baby around," she highlights.

I tilt my head to the side and bring Summer close. "It doesn't seem to bother me. I'm not used to all this domesticated stuff. Yet today wasn't what I thought it would be, and I doubt tomorrow will be, either. We're supposed to be like this, you and me."

"Perhaps. I think we're still getting used to life being not this a few weeks ago and now here we are. A cosmic boom."

I begin to tickle her, and she giggles. "Enough sentimental crap. If you want a cosmic boom, then get on your hands and knees so I can take you from behind." Summer actually listens and begins to stir in my arms, and my cock is already twitching for her.

But alas, that window of opportunity she mentioned seems to hit us right on cue.

We both pause and wait for Bo's crackly sounds to intensify.

Summer growls. "See?" she whispers loudly to me and begins to scoot to the edge of the bed.

I tug her arm to stop her from leaving. "I'll go."

She squinches her eyes. "It's fine, I'm used to—"

Ignoring her, I move to stand. "That's exactly why. Enjoy staying in bed, you dirty girl. I would say clean up, but I kind of have plans for you later."

Summer sighs and squirms to get in a comfortable position. "I shall be waiting. And thank you. Bo is already used to you, so it shouldn't take long to get him back to sleep."

I throw on a shirt, and I'm calm, needing no pep talk. This parenting thing isn't so bad. I think I'm a natural or want to be for them. That's a good thing too, because this is the whole point of me being back in Lake Spark. To help with my brother's widow and his son.

And apparently to stay.

———

Maybe we've settled into a routine. That's what the past week has felt like. My nephew slides an entire bowl of yogurt off his highchair tray onto the floor, and I give him an unimpressed look which only makes him giggle.

Luckily, the babysitter knocks on the front door, and I'm quick to leave Bo in his happy mess to go answer the door for Dana, our babysitter.

"Morning, you're in for a real treat today with Bo. He woke up full of mischief."

She smiles brightly. "That's okay. Makes it more fun."

We make our way back to the kitchen, and I take note of the time on my watch. I was hoping to run a few errands and also knock on Holden's door to see if there is anything I can do. Bo for sure keeps me busy, but in terms of professional work, it seems I have an itch to find something to occupy my time.

My eyes swipe up to Dana who is already making funny voices with Bo as she picks up the bowl.

"I can do that," I offer.

"No worries. Is Summer around? I wanted to ask if I can take a day off next week since I have midterms."

I wave it off. "It's fine. I'm here." The babysitter gives me a peculiar look, or hesitation. "Really, I can be in charge," I assure her, and she has an unnerving smile. I guess she is used to only Summer as her boss, even though she's already seen me a few times.

The thumping down the stairs informs me that Summer must be dressed and ready for her day. We used the snooze button a few too many times for other activities.

Walking down the hall, I meet her at the bottom of stairs.

"I'm so late." She's frantic as she ties her hair up.

"You're fine. I know your boss," I attempt to joke as I slide her coat off the hook by the front door.

Her eyes bug out, and she's displeased. "How many times do I had to tell you that I hate that joke?"

I place my hand on her shoulder to ease her. "But seriously, slow down."

She's already buttoning her coat, ignoring my touch. "I just don't want anyone to think that I'm distracted and dropping the ball. The sympathy card needs to be burned; I hate it."

Leaning down, I swoop up her scarf that she dropped. I swing the fabric around her neck and pull her to me, giving her no choice but to catch a breath. "You're fine. I may have only been back for a short time, but even I know that you still have time to grab a coffee to-go at Jolly Joe's."

Her stern look with her eyes narrowing is cute, but I'd

rather she throws that look at me when I have her on her knees later. For now, I yank her closer to give her a kiss. "May I kiss you good morning to calm you?"

Summer relaxes for a beat and hooks her arms around my neck. "That's not what we're doing. The whole 'have a good day, dear. Don't forget I'm making you lasagna for dinner, so be home on time, dear.'" She throws on a theatrical voice.

"Wait for me naked in bed by eight with your mouth ready, dear," I mumble into her forehead as my lips are planted on her skin.

She pinches me for that remark, but she still lets me kiss her, and a deep one, too.

That is until a sound causes her to flinch right off me, and she straightens her coat. My eyes sideline, and I see Dana holding Bo.

"Uh, I was just… going to change Bo." The poor college kid appears to be a deer in headlights. She wasn't expecting to walk in on this.

"It's… it's fine. Nash was helping me with my scarf," Summer explains, flustered and avoiding eye contact with anyone.

A stiff silence hits all of us.

"I will be home on time today since I know you're preparing for your exams." Summer is quick to kiss the top of Bo's head before she bounces her eyes to study all of us. "Okay, bye." She nearly bolts out the door.

I smile tightly to Dana. "I'm just going to…" I point outside. Dana nods once and doesn't seem to judge and continues with Bo upstairs.

Turning on my heel, I'm quick to catch up with Summer outside where she drops her key fob by her car door and is completely agitated.

"Are you okay?" I cup her elbow as she straightens her body and takes a deep breath with her back to me.

"*No*, Nash. I'm not okay." She turns to face me with complete helplessness. "I meant what I said. How you and I are behind closed doors is for us. In the real world... well, I'm still a widow whose husband has only been gone for a few months."

Pinching my nose, I look past her shoulder to consider my words. "Summer—"

"Nash." Summer peers shyly up at me. "We've hidden our relationship before, we're pros at it."

My eyes grow bold. "That's not the same. Things are different."

She bobs her head side to side. "Under the radar. It's not crazy. We talked about this."

"I understand, but back there was the babysitter who I think could care less."

She now appears fuming. "Do you not remember how small Lake Spark is? It takes one whisper and the whole town will know that I'm sleeping with my dead husband's brother. I mean, what the hell will your parents even think if they find out?"

My lips roll in as I digest her words, and I hold my palms in front of my chest to indicate for her to calm down. "I hear you, I do. Just don't let this ruin your day."

"You're far too relaxed about all of this, but even I know that you want to honor Zac's memory, even if we don't in private."

Her words hit hard. If only she knew how deep we're in.

I swallow any response because I don't have one. "I think we're both on the same page, just coping differently. Now breathe, Summer. You don't have to be perfect."

Her nostrils flare from her hitched breath as she soaks in my words. "I'm sorry. I didn't sleep much last night."

My brows rise and then drop. We both realize why, but this isn't a time to flirt.

"I'll see you later. I really need to go, and I keep reminding myself one day at a time, and today this is where we are," she states as she pulls the handle on the driver's door.

I smile faintly.

Inside, I want to punch something, because I hate that despite what's transpiring between us, she feels a turmoil that's hard to ignore.

———

"CUT THE CRAP. What the fuck have you done?" I say to my brother's gravestone.

It's my first time here since the funeral a few months back. I'm not sure why I haven't visited since, but I can't hold it in anymore.

"Is this some game that you decided we could all play as a parting gift?" I struggle to keep my rage at bay. "There is no way you had me return to Lake Spark under the ruse of watching out for Summer and Bo. I'm just not sure Summer really grasps that. Quite frankly, I'm going to let her figure it out herself. It's the safest way."

Fumbling with loose grass, I sigh as I calm. "I'm attached. To Bo, to Summer, to Lake Spark and its near cult-like fascination with fall. Even the Dizzy Duck, which I had zero interest in before, is suddenly appealing. You were lucky. Lake Spark, the wife, and a son. If only I had realized that, maybe I could have been lucky, too." I toss the grass to the side. "I feel guilty even thinking that. She was always supposed to be yours, but now I realize that it might not be true. I can't have that thought, because otherwise, there would be no Bo. When I came back to Lake Spark, I thought you sent me into this scenario to taunt me with what you had. But is it a taunt if I get it?"

Because that's the kind of man that I am—selfish.

"I'm sorry. This road that you're sending us on? It's not your ridiculous video game of throwing newspapers into people's windows... which by the way, I played all the way through one weekend when you were away with a friend, *and* I beat your high score... It's just... you're playing with us. Except... only I'm aware of the rules to this game it seems."

My sharp breath informs me that I'll only go in a circle. I've said my piece, and now I just need to wait.

———

Tossing a puck between my hands, I lean against Holden's office door, listening to him repeat that everything is under control at the Dizzy Duck.

"Nothing that you need help with?"

Holden seems exhausted from me as he leans back in his chair and chews on a pen. "Just listen when we talk numbers and throw in a few good ideas."

My eyes squint as I study him and realize Summer's conundrum. "You're being extra sensitive and sympathetic to me, aren't you? Don't want me to feel compelled to do more?"

Holden's jaw flexes side to side, as he's aware he has been caught out. "Don't kill me for trying to be a decent human. Summer already makes me question if acting business as usual is normal."

I throw the puck in the air then catch it. "Maybe it is. Just let us figure it out."

"Us?" His face is puzzled.

"I mean the whole mourning someone close to you thing," I correct, and although true, it's not what I meant, and Holden isn't blind, nor will he press.

Holden drops the pen onto this desk and brings his hands behind his head to lean back into the chair. "You know Lake Spark Academy is looking for a new hockey coach, maybe that's something for you."

I laugh instantly. "Coaching teenagers?"

Holden doesn't change his demeanor. "You do realize that most of them end up on great college teams or even straight to major and minor teams when they're eighteen, just like you did, right?"

Throwing the puck his way, he catches it with one hand. "Why would you suggest it if I'm only supposed to be here six weeks?" Possibly because it's obvious that I will be staying longer.

He chuckles under his breath. "Sure." He doubts me, which means he's well aware of my current situation.

"See ya." I decide leaving is the best option, and it causes him to smirk.

I head straight to the lobby, even though I know that Summer is probably already on her way home for Bo.

The lobby is quiet, one of the joys of having a boutique hotel that caters to adults. Everything is always tranquil.

"Hi, Nash, fresh cookie?" Stuart offers from the basket behind the counter with his signature wide smile, as a guest in a suit with their back to me is busy signing a paper.

"Is it ghost-shaped?" I ask in passing as I continue my pace.

"Yes."

"Then fuck no," I call out my response.

I'm nearly one foot out the door when I'm interrupted.

"Aren't you going to say hi, Nash?" I hear.

Oh shit, I know that voice.

I reluctantly turn to see our new Dizzy Duck guest setting the pen down on the counter then grab a cookie from the basket. He turns, clearly happy that he caught me off guard. By the look on his face, he still seems to have me low on his list of favorite people.

"Keats," I greet Summer's brother.

He casually takes a bite of his cookie. "Yep. Thought I would surprise my little sister and see that she's hanging in there."

I rub my forehead, feeling a headache coming on strong. My mind is already contriving how his presence will freak out Summer even more considering our current predicament.

"It's been a while," I say as I drag my thumb across my jaw, unsure of what else to say.

Keats has a smirk laced with confidence that makes even me uneasy, and I've had my fair share of rumbles on the ice. "It has, since you vanished as fast as a breeze after the funeral. Not sure you even spoke to anybody, including my grieving sister."

I take a sharp breath, tamping down the urge to snap back. "Summer didn't mention that you would be in town."

He hasn't blinked once due to his unwavering thoughts. "She isn't aware that I'm here. I thought I would visit to check up on her and my nephew. If I told her my plans, then she would just protest and say she's fine," he explains, and it feels as though we are already in a stare-off.

"I'm sure she'll…"

"A word." Keats indicates with his head to follow him as he brushes past me. Dread hits me, as nothing about Keats feels promising when it comes to me. He turns when we are out on the veranda with rocking chairs. "She mentioned that you moved in temporarily."

"I did. It was Zac's request."

He scoffs. "I'm sure it's only causing more turmoil for my sister."

I stand tall, and my nose rises slightly to square off. "Why would you say that?"

He seems humored by me. "The thing is… Summer and your brother were always close. They made sense and had a good marriage with a beautiful baby. You? You're like a tornado rolling into town and uprooting my sister's life. So, I don't care what the fuck was in your brother's mind about this little arrangement, but I can guarantee that Summer is not getting space to process and grieve."

Gently I shake my head in disbelief. "What is it that you hate about me so much? You've made no effort to hide it."

Keats's eyes grow into saucers in surprise. "You were a cocky asshole already when you played varsity hockey, but that's not the issue. I'm not an idiot. Ever since the car crash when *you* were driving, my sister could barely muster your name for the past few years, and now suddenly you appear in photos of Bo with pumpkins. So yeah, sorry if brother bear is here to check up."

Licking my lips, I can understand where he's coming from, which is odd, as it's not exactly in my favor. "You're kind of being an ass considering it's my brother who passed."

Keats pauses for a second, a small dose of regret showing in his eyes. "I'm… sorry. I'm just worried about Summer. She's always been one to appear okay on the outside while breaking on the inside."

I couldn't agree more, and I hate that she and I are an unsettling feeling of right and wrong. Swallowing, I do my best to be careful with my words. "I'm doing my best to look out for her. To ensure she and Bo are okay."

There is skepticism written all over Keats's face as he

leans against the pillar and crosses his arms. "I'm seriously wondering how that's working."

Glancing up, I'm still uneasy of what exactly Keats's theory may be in his head, but I'm going to bury it and do what is best for Summer. "I think it's a good idea that you let Summer know you're in town, and I'm sure you must be excited to see Bo, too."

"Very true." He tugs up his sleeve to peek at his watch. "Since you're living with my sister, then I'm sure you can confirm that Bo still goes to bed around seven, which means I need to get a move on to see them."

My jaw tightens. "Schedule confirmed."

Keats strolls away slowly, patting my shoulder in passing. "I'm only being an ass because it's my sister on the line, and I worry about her." There is honesty in his voice, which I do appreciate.

Still, just as he has doubts about me, I have misgivings about his presence.

———

Bo sits on Keats's knee, and they stare at one another. "You're getting big too fast. Slow it down."

I'm observing from the sofa with a beer in hand. Summer does seem happy as she sits on the floor near them. "Or you're just not visiting him enough, Mr. Bigshot Lawyer?"

Her brother gives her a pointed look in jest. "I'm not complaining about that title."

"Sure, but I don't see any women trailing behind you, so you may need to work on a few qualities," Summer teases.

Keats quirks his lips at Bo. "Did you hear that? Your mommy is being mean."

"That's the whole point of being a sibling, to watch out and call you out when needed."

Keats's eyes sharply dagger my gaze. Summer's innocent sentence has way too much meaning.

Clearing my throat, I divert us. "The Chinese food should be here soon."

Summer skims a quick look at me before returning to wiggling Bo's feet playfully. "It's the easiest, plus you don't need to cook."

"Sounds like you two have a routine down to the T."

Summer slides her eyes between her brother and me, uncertain how to answer. "Kind of happens when you're living together." She shrugs.

"Well, I'm here for a few days while a crew finish renovations at my house in Everhope, so I can help you out if needed. Stock up on Halloween candy or something ridiculous. Do you need me to check out that sink you were complaining about?" her brother offers, even though he's probably the last person to be able to fix a sink. His life is law and overworking.

"Oh, well, Nash already fixed the sink and bought all the candy we need when we were at the store." Summer smiles, still unaware that her brother wants to roast me.

"All is well," I direct my sentence to only Keats, as Summer focuses on Bo.

His cheeks twitch with his eyes darkening. "Seems so."

"It's really great that you're back in Lake Spark for a visit. It feels like it's been forever since I've seen you," she mentions.

Keats bounces Bo on his knee and plays with his little arms. "I'll be around more as I will handling legal for the Spinners. Anyhow, you know I'm always just a phone call away, and I should have visited more, but you were kind of persistent that having space to return to normalcy has been helping."

Summer looks in my direction for a millisecond. "I thought so," she says softly.

A silence overcomes us as we all accept the fact that Summer had it all wrong.

Keats thinks she's admitting to needing more support.

And I believe it's because she needs me.

Keats wanders his eyes around him then picks up the stuffed monkey. "This is the weirdest monkey ever."

"It's a proboscis monkey," I clarify.

Summer snorts a laugh. "Nash got it for Bo when he was born, and Bo won't sleep without it."

Yet again, Keats shoots his eyes between Summer and me.

Luckily, I'm saved by the doorbell. "I'll get that."

"We'll head into the kitchen," Summer says and already begins to shuffle on the floor.

I head to the door and answer to collect the bag of food. I double-check the receipt stapled to the paper bag to ensure that we have the right order, thank the delivery man with a tip, and make my way to the kitchen where Summer is buckling Bo into his chair.

"Mashed avocado?" I ask her, and she throws me an appreciative look as I set the food on the table. Like our normal routine, I grab an avocado from the fruit bowl and get to work on getting Bo's plate ready.

"Oh, can you get his bib? I think the blue one is clean," she requests.

Picking up the bib by the sink, I raise it in the air. "Got it."

I can't help noticing that Keats is studying us intently as Summer and I work together in our new rhythm that is our evening routine. It's a minute later when we're settled at the table.

"Make yourself useful and unpack the boxes," Summer goads her brother.

They've always been close in their own sort of way. As much as Keats's sharp stare is unnerving, he's making Summer appear lighter today. She's smiling more than normal.

"How's Everhope?" I'm putting in the effort to make conversation.

At last, Keats seem to ease. "I think I like it. My house is almost ready, and right now my neighbor's house is empty, so I have extra privacy. Someone won't be moving in for another few months. There is a lot of space in my house, too. A few bedrooms too many, and I'm desperate for a house-guest with a baby. Hint, hint."

Summer is busy loading her plate and doesn't look up. "You've mentioned a few times."

"You already turned down my offer to move out of Lake Spark for a change of scene," he reminds Summer.

Her tongue darts to the corner of her mouth. "I have this house, and Zac would have wanted me to live here. I can't run. It won't change that he's gone."

The air evaporates from the room, and the only sound is in the background, Bo making muffled noises with his spoon.

I bring my hand to rest on the nape of my neck, realizing that when I least expect it something slices into me. It seems that this is one of those times.

"Summer." His voice is near authoritarian because he noticed that Summer's mood dropped. Keats places his hand on her arm to comfort her. "It's okay. It will get better." She rips her arm away from his grasp and abruptly stands to leave the table and flee the room.

Keats immediately sighs and realizes his error. "I should go fin—"

"No. I'll do it," I cut in, and my palm indicates for him to stay put. To my surprise he seems to agree.

Leaving Bo and Keats in the kitchen, I don't need to search where Summer is as I know she's upstairs, probably pacing in front of Bo's room. That's her spot when she's upset. I skip steps to get to her faster, and despite her back to me, I already know when she turns that tears will be pooling in her eyes.

"Summer."

"Nash." I don't even get a chance to view her face before she buries into my chest with my arms looping around her.

"He was just trying to help."

Her quiet cry is killing me, and her puffy eyes that slides up to me don't help. "I know. He's always done everything to be there for me. I just feel guilty because the only thing that seems to be helping is..." She hiccups a sniffle. "You."

I soothe her back and bring her to my chest. Her favorite pillow, even if it's soaked in tears. Kissing the top of her head, I'm conflicted, too. "We're figuring it out," I assure her.

"He wouldn't see it that way. It's a constant battle of following what everyone expects but wanting to scream that there is another way that's helping me. Gluing tiny pieces together. It's fucked up too, because it's only been a few weeks since you've been here, and we were quick to fall into one another's arms."

My body tightens, reminding myself that I'm in this with her, and we'll unravel to where we are supposed to end up. "Summer, you just have to… Our little world, remember that, okay? For now, that's what helps, and in time it might make sense."

Summer reluctantly nods and grips my shirt to ensure she

can't let go with our eyes, confirming that we need one another.

The sound of steps startles Summer, and she steps back to smooth her hair.

"Sorry." Her brother is holding Bo and seems to struggle with words. "Bo seems to need a new diaper."

Summer wipes away a tear with her wrist. "I'll just take him straight to bed. It's time anyway. Besides, I'd rather do that than listen to you grill me about why I'm crying."

Keats hands over the baby to Summer with sympathy etched on his face. "I was going to let you off the hook tonight. Plus…" His eyes brush a quick glance in my direction. "It seems you don't need me for that."

Protectively, Summer holds Bo tight to her body and kisses his cheek. "Just go downstairs and eat before it gets cold."

"Stop being a pain in my ass and not eating your dinner. It's not even peas, it's a warm eggroll calling your name," he rebuffs.

Keats is fond of her, and their back-and-forth is something that Zac and I used to have. Maybe a twinge of jealousy hits me that Summer still gets that with someone.

We both let Summer escape, and Keats and I share a look of understanding.

We even sit in silence while we attempt to eat. I guess we'll be adding more leftovers for tomorrow.

"Be honest with me. You and Summer are more than roommates." His eyes remain fixed on his fork, playing with his food. "It's obvious."

I collapse in my chair because apparently my body was tense walking on eggshells.

He continues, "Here's the thing. If it helps her smile

again, then fine. But just remember that it's easy for her to be confused right now. Once the cloud clears, then what?"

Biting my inner cheek, I'm doubting whether I'm in the hot seat or being offered an olive branch. "What if she is the one also clearing my cloud?" I challenge.

It grabs Keats's attention, and he doesn't blink as our eyes meet. He doesn't answer me. Instead, he stands. "Tell Summer that I'll see her tomorrow morning for breakfast at the Dizzy Duck."

"Okay," I promise.

"Just her and me." His tone is short.

I stay quiet and give him a weak salute as he walks past me, before both of my hands come to my face, and I laugh bitterly to myself.

————

We sit in the middle of the bed with Summer's legs wrapped around me as she sits in my lap. I can't stop caressing her cheek, her scar, her hair, brushing kisses everywhere I can without breaking our embrace. We're naked and tied up with a blanket around our middle; it seems like we've been here for a long time, and perhaps we have.

Summer drops her head to my shoulder. "Tell me something happy."

"Hmm, where should I begin?"

"A memory."

My lips stretch as I recall one. "You used to love these chips, sour cream and onion. It was after one of my game days at the end of the season, and we were going to watch a movie on my couch. I think we were making out or something, but when you laid back, there was a bag of your chips, and you completely flattened them. Your back was covered in that sour-cream-and-onion smell. It was all over my sofa, and it took like weeks to get that smell out. Your shirt was completely ruined and had to go into the washing machine." I chuckle under my breath.

She smiles against my skin. "Then you gave me one of your shirts to wear and… it was the same one you gave me when I was eighteen. You didn't even realize."

"I guess I didn't. Just habit, maybe."

Her lips drag along the curve of my shoulder. "This is a horrible idea. Memory lane keeps us swirling back to the idea of a different road."

My fingers draw lazy circles on her back. "Fine. Holden suggested I apply to be the new hockey coach at Lake Spark Academy."

Immediately, she giggles a laugh. "That's funny," she sputters out. "I just can't see you hanging around your old stomping ground and dealing with high-strung parents. Besides, would you even pass the background check? You literally pulled a prank every week when you were there."

"Hey, filling the principal's office with a bubble machine was a smart idea… we just underestimated the soap residue not coming off wood so easily."

She squeezes and shakes my shoulder. "You got away with so much shit. No way were they going to get rid of you. They needed your skills to win regionals."

"When you have a gift, use it," I say cockily.

"I made a cake and dropped a beer bottle cap into the batter. Only realized that after it was in the oven."

I laugh. "Oh yeah, in high school. We decided it was either break the cake open or eat it and see who got the lucky piece. You ended up with the bottle cap slice."

"It was a good luck charm and saved my ass from my

parents discovering it. I think Keats had a party or something. I'm not sure, but we said whoever got the piece was lucky."

"You are. It just seems blurry right now."

Summer's lips press together, but she doesn't answer. I shouldn't have said that. It's all wrong.

I take her with me when I lie back down. "You're going to be okay tomorrow with your brother?"

"It's fine. If things feel like they're going south, I will just shove a croissant into my mouth."

"Just stay clear of the pumpkin-shaped platter." Her face turns perplexed. "It means there is an edible ghost shape somewhere in the vicinity."

She seems to think that I'm being ridiculous, and I am joking, partly. Summer bops my nose with hers. "Aren't you cute."

"Some of the time. Others would say that I'm grumpy or an ass the rest of the time."

"That's okay. Only I get to see your other side, which is good, as it involves a lot of commands and lack of clothing." Her sexy look is going to get us in trouble, but her eyes soften. "You have a side that surprises me as much as you. You're not the same anymore. Just seeing you with Bo I realize that."

I wrap my arms firmly around her. "And when it comes to you? Am I the same?"

It's a long silence then a sigh. "No. We've been dealt a hand in life that has made us resilient, and it only works if we have one another. It's as exhilarating as it is scary."

"Tunnels. You go in one side and leave the other. Sometimes you don't know what's on the other side."

Except I do. And if Summer is scared, then she might be petrified.

SUMMER

Throwing a piece of croissant at my brother, I'm reminded how Keats has always been the brother who can still alleviate a bad day, even if he has ideas in his head that he will never change his mind about.

His gleaming brown eyes accompanied by his grin cause me to wonder why my handsome brother's parade of women hasn't yet led to finding the one.

But I have a feeling that this breakfast won't be about him for even a second.

My brother winces when the piece of croissant hits his chest. "Chill out, Summer." He smirks as he grabs his cup of coffee. We're sitting by the window of the Dizzy Duck's restaurant for breakfast. I'm not starting work until later, so it's refreshing to just sit here without obligations.

"You asked me how I am again. Not the how am I as in the answer is good, but the *how am I,* as in am I having a breakdown yet."

Keats gawks his eyes at me. "And? It's not a crime."

I puff out an exhausted breath. "Can we talk about something else? I want to say it's great seeing you, and it's great for Bo, but I'm sure the underlying reason of why you're here will only piss me off again, and my eggs haven't even arrived yet." I rip off another piece of croissant as I sink back in my seat.

"Fine. I needed to use some vacation days."

I snort a laugh. "You don't take vacations and probably already woke at the crack of dawn to work on your laptop."

"Maybe I've changed."

"Doubt it."

He tips his cup in my direction. "Bad cover, huh?"

"Could have thought of a few better reasons."

He sighs and is about to say something, but Jane, our waitress, appears with our plates of eggs and bacon. We both thank her, and when she leaves, Keats seems ready to pick up where he left off.

"I promise I'll focus on Bo talk in a minute, but first, I need to talk about something." He doesn't even look up as he sprinkles pepper on his eggs.

I give up and set my fork on the edge of the plate, shaking my head as I'm defeated. "Say it."

Keats examines me for a few seconds. "Nash," he states simply.

A breath gets trapped in my chest before I let go. "What about him?"

My brother's eyes impale me to let me know that he is serious, with zero ounce of humor about to come my way. "He's more than your house guest."

A weak laugh leaves me. "Of course, he's Bo's uncle."

Keats gives me a pointed look, clearly not believing me. "I'm not blind."

My eyes circle the room, ensuring that nobody is about to hear that my brother is going to tell me his unwelcome wisdom.

"He was just comforting me last night, it happens some-times." Keats still isn't buying it. "I'm not going to talk about this with you."

"Oh, you are." His tone is firm, and my eyes nearly pop out. "You're vulnerable, and I don't want this to blow up in your face when you process your emotions at a later date."

"You don't get to say what I need to cope," I counter.

Keats throws his napkin onto the table and slides his plate to the side with a jostled sound of his fork before he rests his elbows on the table. "Exactly, I don't. If you would let me finish, then you might also realize that I accept that your current life chapter is up to you about how you want to deal with it."

"Just not with Nash," I bite back.

A smirk begins to stretch on my brother's mouth which surprises me. "To my own disbelief, I'm not saying that."

My neck gooses up, curious what point he is trying to make. "Then what are you saying?"

"I want to say he's taking advantage of your sadness right now, but on this visit to Lake Spark, you seem a tad brighter, and that's new. And…" His tongue glides along his teeth before he scratches his neck, preparing himself to finish the sentence. "I have to find some compassion that he lost someone too, and it seems you are also helping him find his way."

My eyes narrow in on my brother, and my body tenses because this isn't Keats. I'm fairly confident that his coldness toward Nash didn't fade overnight. "Why are you being empathetic?"

He snickers while he quickly glances out the bay window to the calm lake with orange and yellow leaves surrounding the trees that outline the water. Then his sight lands right back on me with a nearly smug look. "The thing is… I've always seen it. Not just now. It's always been there."

My shoulders sag, and I shake my head gently, informing him that I have no clue and am waiting for his explanation.

"You and Zac made sense. But the Nix brothers have always had something in common. Zac and Nash looked at you the same way, madly in love with you." My eyes drop at his admission. "But you only ever had the same look for one of them… Nash."

Snapping up my eyes, I'm surprised by his observation, but internally, I've always felt it. It's just I never expected someone to say it so bluntly.

"Why are you telling me this?"

Keats reaches across the table to touch the top of my hand. "Because I also know that your loss is now turning into turmoil because of that simple fact. You think you're not following the rule book. Too soon, wrong person, not honorable, and all that other shit that gets put in our heads."

My throat tightens by his views because they are spot on. "It's only been a few months and…"

He pats my hand before he returns to sitting up straight. "Trust me." His brows knit together. "That crossed my mind."

"Then imagine what other people might think." The building of frustration and guilt begin to swirl up inside me.

"I'm not here to say that's going to be okay. I can't. However, I do think someone needs to tell you that's it's okay to eventually move on, and maybe that's now or not. Just… you are."

Widening my eyes to keep tears down, I appreciate his encouragement. "I'm not sure what to say. I wasn't expecting the conversation to go this way."

He chuckles and adjusts his plate in front of him. "Trust me, yesterday I wouldn't have expected it either. It's just, you are my kid sister, and whatever sliver it may take to ease your pain, I'll allow it."

I laugh. "Allow it? I swear to God, this whole honorable-brother philosophy that everyone in Lake Spark possesses is making me question the water here."

"So what? It has me sitting in front of you, telling you that you can do all this in your own way. Being sad for life isn't what Zac would have wanted."

A warmth fills my heart because he's right. I just don't remind myself enough.

I pick up my fork and begin to play with my eggs, and I'm going to be honest. "I just don't know how to handle all of this except to say that Nash is helping." A faint smile cracks the lines on my face. "It's crazy. Sometimes I wonder if Zac did all this on purpose. But that would just be… I'm not sure what it would be."

Keats gives me a knowing glare. "Is it far-fetched?"

Hmm, that hypothesis is so obvious, but still, I'm not ready to commit to the theory.

"Can we move on from this conversation? A sunnier topic, perhaps?" I implore.

Keats beams at me. "You've earned that after listening to me."

"Geez, thanks," I state dryly, and it causes him to chuckle.

"I think I'll leave later today. I'll take Bo to the park and then head out. It seems I don't need to stay a few days to babysit you, and you're doing alright. You have someone stepping in for me."

A warm wry smile naturally appears. "I think so, too."

"Good. Because Bo spit up on my expensive shirt, and I'm not sure I'm in the mood for a repeat and a need to replace my wardrobe," he jokes.

Now comfortable, I get to work on my plate of food.

"Please, oh please," I beg with my hands in prayer, "let me find you a girlfriend. Maybe on one of those apps or see if taking out a newspaper ad will help. One day you might have a child, and then you'll never care about any shirt, you'll see. And if kids aren't for you, then at least you'll have a relationship, and I don't need to learn a new name."

"Watch it there. I can rewind this entire breakfast if you feel like you want to take us back to an uncomfortable discussion," he teases.

I ruefully shake my head. "Shut up and pass me the salt."

I've been lucky. The past few days between Nash and my brother, I've been distracted, as if life is almost whole again. That's a promising start.

Over the remainder of our breakfast, we change topics to his work and our holiday schedules to puzzle a time to get together. It's only when Nash slowly strolls into the dining room, eyeing us, unsure of the atmosphere, that I'm reminded I need to work soon.

"Hey," I greet him.

"I was with Stone, checking on something for the Dizzy Duck, and thought I would stop by." Nash stares at Keats with caution which now nearly makes me laugh.

It's only a solid ten seconds of silence before my brother pulls out his chair and stands. "Well, I think I need to get a move on. Just let the babysitter know I'm stopping by to hang with my nephew for an hour."

I stand too and nervously play with my hair. "Of course."

Keats and Nash give one another a nod, and when my brother offers his hand to Nash, confusion floods Nash's face, but he reluctantly shakes his hand. A strong shake, a shake of truce, and it's kind of touching.

"Take care of her," my brother warns Nash.

"You don't need to tell me," Nash reminds him softly.

"*And* that's my cue to break up this little strange initiation." I do my best to use a cheerful tone.

Their hands drop, and my brother gives me one last knowing smile before stepping to me for a quick hug. "Remember what I said," he whispers.

I nod in understanding.

Nash observes from the sidelines as my brother walks away. We both watch Keats's every step until he vanishes.

"What the fuck was that? Did I miss the apocalypse?" Nash is mesmerized after the last minute, then he directs his stare to me.

"My brother just gave me a little insight." I hope that my lack of a frown eases Nash, especially when I touch his arm. "Maybe later we can talk? I need to check in with the event planner for someone's wedding this weekend."

His hand mirrors my gesture and grazes my arm for a quick touch. "Of course. You're all good?"

My smile is authentic with no need to cover my internal demons. "I think so."

———

LEANING against the kitchen counter with a glass of wine in hand, my eyes follow Nash's path as he enters the room and heads straight to the fridge. He put Bo to bed tonight.

"Have I mentioned lately that your baby-whisperer skills have been upgraded to an eight?"

Nash peeks out from around the open fridge door. "Oh yeah?" He's proud.

"Uh-oh, I just boosted your self-image."

He closes the door with a beer bottle in his hand, then he slides the bottle opener that was lying on the counter off, snaps the cap, and throws the cap somewhere near the sink, which he most definitely will be picking up later. Arriving next to me, he joins in leaning over the counter and looking in the same direction toward the wall where a picture of me hangs, taken one fall day. It was spontaneous, but I think the way the light catches my eyes and glimmers on my skin makes me confidently beautiful.

Somehow, similar to many family photos in this house, everything became part of the background, and I forget to look. Today, the remnants of other times give me a few moments of self-reflection for my body to relax.

"We never got to talk about your brother. Is he always so brazen or just when I'm around?"

I grin as I nudge Nash's shoulder with mine. "Actually, he gave me a little perspective, and no, he took you off his list of who to hunt down. Not sure he was praising your graces, but it was close enough."

"Really?"

I nod once. "He knows about us. Or at least, his own notion of us. To my surprise, we talked, and he gave me a little hope that I don't need to feel so guilty as long as this is right."

Nash's eyes nearly bug out when I side-eye him. "And do you believe in what you just said?"

The balls of my bare feet turn on the smooth wood to rest my back against the counter. "Maybe a tiny bit."

Nash moves to stand in front of me with my legs between his as we stand, and both of his hands rest on the counter to frame my hips, giving me a chance to leave. But I don't want to. The heat between us and the subtle hint of a cardamom-pine cologne hits my senses.

"I'm happy if his unexpected visit gave you a little peace of mind."

My lips quirk out, and my fingers find his shirt to play

with. "I think I'm going to let go of a little guilt. Otherwise, it only prolongs the sorrow, doesn't it?"

Nash releases one of his hands and runs his long finger along my cheek. "I believe so."

"I can breathe a little more easily after talking to him. I thought he would judge me, and maybe he was, but in the end, he made me feel that I'm finding my own way, and I shouldn't be scared about others' expectations of what I should feel."

"Summer, it's true."

Collecting his finger in my hand, I bring it up to my lips for a soft kiss. "It's still not entirely clear what we're doing, Nash. But I'm choosing to go to sleep with a little less remorse, and that already lifts me a little more."

Something I say sets him off because he scoops my head into his hands at record speed, and his mouth lowers to capture my lips in a firm kiss filled with reverence. "I needed to hear you say that." Nash kisses my forehead then pulls me in tight to his chest.

My mouth tugs as it seems we are standing in the same place and not just literally.

I pull away, and our eyes dance in recognition of where we are in life. There is a glint in Nash's eyes that holds me. I can't tear away from them, even when he hoists me up onto the kitchen counter with clear purpose for what he wants.

"Summer," he rasps.

I press my finger against his lips. "Shh."

The corner of his mouth hitches up before he continues his journey, leading me to lie on my back as his mouth travels down my body, stopping just above that sensitive spot. Instead, he kisses my belly and then again.

"Screw my shh plea, I need to tell you that doing this on the kitchen counter is wildly inappropriate considering there are baby bottles and cereal crumbs scattered around the counter," I joke to break our moment into bliss.

"Tsk, tsk," Nash tuts. "All the more incentive to take this wildly inappropriateness onto the floor." In a flash, he picks me up, and we fall to the floor, and I giggle as we stumble. But he wastes no time and gets me on my back with his teeth dragging my shirt up, tugging a few times, his stubbled jaw rubbing against my skin and causing a sensitive ripple in my body.

I moan purely from watching him and his persistence. He must notice. "You might have back pain tomorrow. I need to keep you on the floor for a while so I can go slow and take you the way you deserve since you've knocked down a brick or two."

As tempting as that is… I push him off me, and he sinks to sitting with his back to the cupboard door. I end up in his lap with my legs around him. "That's only if you manage to get me off of you," I challenge him, and I sweep my shirt up and off.

This is a mixture of fun and passion that continues to grow between us. There is a reason I don't look at the pictures around the house anymore.

Because Nash re-entered my life, causing me to be blinded of the border between past and present.

NASH

With her hands on her hips and eyes wide, Summer stands in the living room like a super-woman. She's surprised, but it's already making her beam a smile.

"This is the costume choice?"

Bouncing Bo in my arms, he gives me no animation because he's probably wondering what the fuck I've done to him.

"He's a little hockey player," I explain proudly.

"I gathered that with the booties that look like skates and a jersey, and is that a helmet? Wait, is that like a plush hockey stick?"

Glancing down, I admit that I knocked this out of the park. The onesie jersey might be a pain in the ass if we have a diaper drama.

Summer walks to Bo and instantly makes little noises with him, the type where she raises her tone and has a melody.

"I think everyone will think you are the cutest baby, yes you are." She pretends to bite his skate, and he squeals.

"Does this upgrade me on the baby-qualification scale?"

Summer pretends to contemplate with her finger on her chin. "Hmm, let me think. You did pick his costume and now know how to make his bottle… If you can make his mom relax by coming a little more during the night, then that might get you those extra points."

My jaw drops, because even if she's toying with me, she just crossed a line. "Whoa there, my ability to relax you has a higher point average than my baby-scale record."

She has a sultry appearance on her face, and I like that a lot. "You're right. I'll give you a 9.5. Now we should head to the Dizzy Duck staff party."

"What are the chances that I can pass off the baby and sneak off with you?"

Summer nearly frowns. "I think as much as I'm taking my fears down a notch… I think we need to—"

"I agree. Relax," I assure her.

"Good. Now let's go stuff our faces with food so we don't need to worry about dinner later."

I attempt to grab Bo's attention. "See? Your mom is a smart lady."

It's a half-hour later when we get to the Dizzy Duck. Staff are busy out back enjoying a buffet and carving pumpkins. The weather is perfect today. An afternoon that only requires a light jacket. A few clouds, but I always felt autumn isn't a sunny season.

Summer gently cups my elbow as we arrive and takes Bo from my arms. "I'm going to catch up with Lexi and Harlow, plus they are near the caramel-apple-making station, and that's kind of my priority today." It makes me happy that she's already loving her day.

I mosey my way to Stone and Holden who are standing on the patio near the bench swing and a bit away from everyone, looking out at the lake, both with drinks in their hands. They greet me as I join them.

"Shouldn't we be more social?"

Holden partly turns his shoulder with a feigned attempt to check. "My kids are chill, so no, I'm not going to interrupt my moment of solitude," he states dryly before taking a sip of his beer. His pre-teen and teenager can get a little rambunctious at times.

Stone takes a long sip from his beer then makes a noise, informing me that it's a good IPA. "The women are gossiping, and there's a baby present. We're all good."

I chuckle at their answers. "Alright."

Holden tips his nose in the direction of Summer holding Bo. "Cute costume." While he means it, I sense the undertone.

"Something you care to share?"

Stone and Holden exchange awkward glances, and it seems Stone is the one to take the plunge. "He is cute, really. It's just… the arrangement between you and Summer. We're all trying to get used to you stepping into Zac's shoes… and…" He sounds uncomfortable as he scratches his cheek, and his eyes plead with Holden for a save.

"Fuck it." Holden hangs his beer bottle low with his fingers. "Is there something more going on? There. We said it."

My body constricts, and suddenly I'm having déjà vu as this keeps happening lately, and every time I grasp where Summer is coming from. "What's it to anyone if there is?"

Again, they seem to look to one another for encouragement. "It's not our business as long as Summer ends up in a better place. You kind of missed the immediate aftermath of your brother passing and watching Summer try to cope before jumping into acting as though nothing happened." That reminder is not appreciated because it twists me. "Don't get us wrong. It's great seeing her in better spirits. It's just sometimes everything happens so fast that you don't realize until after."

My eyes bug out and my lips pop out. "Not your business but still offering your thoughts. Thanks." I'm not exactly impressed.

"Don't lose it. That's our view, and we can move on. We care for Summer, that's all."

"Way to go on making this a festive staff celebration," I say sarcastically.

Stone slants his head to the side for a second. "To be fair, the party favors are kind of above par."

A contrite smile grows on my mouth. "Aren't you two adorable."

They smirk to themselves. "We are. Now, we are happy that you survived Keats and also Summer doesn't have a fake smile on her face for once. Which reminds me, did she tell you about our guest yesterday?" Holden asks.

"No." It's nice that we can switch gears.

"This guy who is worth millions called the front desk at like one in the morning. You would think he wanted a whiskey or something. Do you know what he wanted?"

Stone takes a guess. "A hooker that doesn't exist in Lake Spark as we are a wholesome town?"

"Nah, he wanted a cheese sandwich cut into animal shapes and a glass of milk."

Stone and I sputter out a laugh. "What?"

"Yeah, and he even wanted a straw in the milk."

"The night receptionist told us about it the next morning in the staff meeting," Holden explains.

"I think when my parents owned this place it was mostly marriage breakups for the world to see. Oh, they had one guy who snuck in a fifty-pound lizard, and it got loose."

"Your parents also had that ridiculous moose on the wall," Stone reminds me. Luckily, last year they ditched the dead animal for a different interior design.

Fondly, I smile. "Old school."

"No offence, our new direction of the Dizzy Duck just ups the standard." Holden is proud of this place, as he should be since he puts in the most hours.

"By the way, speaking of guests, did you run into the principal from your kids' school again?" Stone pries.

"Nah, thankfully. I have angels now since Lexi entered the picture with her stepmom-extraordinaire skills."

I wonder if I'm entering the picture as more than an uncle to Bo. Not sure why that thought comes to my mind, but it's a credible question.

"Well, I did. She asked if I want to coach the hockey team," Stone explains.

"I'm sure you declined, with your writing schedule." Holden grips my shoulder. "Besides, if Nash sticks around then the job is his."

Shaking my head, I press my lips together. "Not happening."

If I stick around? I need to address that at some point.

"I'm telling Dad that you're texting Justin Russo." Holden's son is loud enough that we hear him snipe at his sister.

Holden recoils. "My clue that peace is broken." He groans and turns, while Stone and I follow as we should probably check on everyone. Besides, I'm getting hungry.

Summer and I meet halfway to the buffet table. The way the breeze blows in her hair gives me a view of her entire neck which is beautiful. Necks are underappreciated.

"Want me to go on duty?" I offer.

She already begins to hand Bo off. "That would be great. I'm dead serious. I need to make a candy apple and down a pumpkin-spiced expresso martini that I hear is rumored to be floating around."

I chortle from the fact that she's not one bit joking. "I might be carrying you both home later," I note.

She waves me off. "Nah, I'm a perfectly responsible adult."

Her high spirits wilt to a frown, and I notice she's looking over my shoulder. I follow her line of sight and instantly relate to where her mind just went. There's a boy who is dressed as a doctor.

And I'm the asshole who chose the hockey costume instead of the doctor option at the store. Bo's dad, the doctor.

"Next year. A perfect costume for Bo." I mean it when I say it.

Summer meets my gaze. "I'm fine. Maybe it's good that sometimes we get little reminders just to ensure he isn't forgotten. For Bo."

She attempts to bring her smile back, but it's weak. "There are sweet potatoes in the buffet. That would be perfect for Bo."

"A gourmet meal is coming his way," I promise.

The glimmer of appreciation in her eyes for the support is only intended for me, we just flow. Summer is about to step closer to show affection to me but stops herself when her eyes circle, and she reminds herself where we are.

It doesn't matter. She's having a decent day, and that's all that matters.

———

"YOU'RE KIND OF TIPSY," I tease Summer as she giggles.

Bo was fast asleep in the car, and I took him straight to bed. Now, I'm downstairs on the couch with Summer and enjoying a drink to kick back and relax.

Summer indicates with her fingers a small size as she sits on her knees and faces me. "A tiny bit. It's been forever since I've enjoyed a cocktail."

I'm entertained. "It's been a while since I've seen this. What does tipsy Summer do again?"

"Eat lots of Halloween candy."

"We'll have nothing left."

"Uhm. I used to strip for you," she recalls.

My lips quirk out as my bottle rests on my lap. She did. That was the thing. We were explosive together. So much so that I feared at times it was only that. But then it was clear.

Summer was more.

She *is* more.

"What else do you remember?" I prod, fully invested that we're in replay mode.

Summer springs up from the couch and offers her hand to me. "You would dance with me."

Setting my beer bottle on the side table, I grin. I have no qualms, if she wants a man that will dance with her, then that is what she'll get.

I smirk as she begins to lead the way, her arms floating as she takes my hands.

"There's no music," I highlight that fact.

Her face softens. "I don't think that matters."

Taking hold of her hands, I bring them to my chest, causing our distance to close as we both begin to sway with our eyes entranced.

The last few minutes of fun and banter vanish as something profound overwhelms the air, nearly creating a catastrophic tension. It takes no words to acknowledge that.

Summer slides her hands around me to hold on as her head lands on my chest.

"You always surprised me. Every time in your arms, I felt more protected than the last." Her tone is neutral, no longer tipsy and thoughts in her head sobering her up.

Kissing the top of her head, I wrap my arms around her as we continue to barely sway. "It's still the case, Summer. I just…" *Let you go.*

"Don't leave me, too." With her somber tone, I can't figure out if she's asking for a promise or telling me a fear.

My breath catches as I come to terms with a reality that I need to make clear. "I'm not going anywhere, Summer."

She doesn't look up nor change her tone. "I forgot that the clock had six weeks on it when it comes to us."

I begin to rub circles on her back. "Did I not make myself clear at the pumpkin patch? I'm breaking the clock. I'm staying."

It causes our eyes to find one another like a magnet. "I've lost my best friend. He isn't coming back. But you? I've lost once, and I won't survive twice."

My hands are quick to frame her face, forcing her gaze to connect with mine. "I promise you. I'm already two steps ahead of you. I won't let you break," I promise her.

"I'm counting on that." The vulnerability is apparent, it's written all over her body.

"Remember? You're my puck." Please bring that smile back again.

She sputters a laugh. "The puck that you fuck. How could I forget."

It does the trick. I won't let her wallow or sink down a spiral because she's sad or scared.

"I said some stupid stuff then," I admit.

The corners of her mouth sweep slightly up. "And I loved

it. We would laugh a lot… I don't want us to be a mess of emotions this time around. We can still laugh, every day I see that more."

"Me too, Summer, me too."

"Can we go upstairs?"

I don't answer her, my droll smile is enough.

We head upstairs, and once we're in her room, there's a shift.

We both find our way to the middle of the bed, on top of the duvet, on our knees, facing each other but watching our fingertips imprint against one another.

"I think the cloud we've been thrown into is beginning to vanish," she comments.

It doesn't take a scientist to be aware that this entire situation of how we ended up here was out of our hands, or at least, this chapter of life. Even if I never let her go, my brother would still be gone.

My mouth lowers to hers, our lips mold, and it's that tender part of me that I only have with her. Our tongues swirl against one another.

"We'll make it to other side of the cloud, I promise."

Then I slowly guide her back until we're lying on top of the mattress, taking time to just say nothing, instead letting our fingers explore.

Her eyes flick up to tie us together with an invisible string. "You've been making a lot of promises lately… but this time I believe you," she whispers.

This is the man I should have been. I recognize that. It's different now.

Because I have more promises to come.

18

—

SUMMER

—

I'm not sure why I'm sitting at Catch 22. Not when I have the Dizzy Duck and Jolly Joe's as the lunch options in town. Instead, I decided to meet Harlow the extra 15-minute walk from Main Street. Sometimes it's nice to have a change of scene, and their chicken salad sandwich is to die for.

"We are too lucky with this fall. I'm sure I just jinxed myself and now we'll have snow for Thanksgiving. I've only lived here for a short while, but I'm now accustomed to the fact that Illinois weather likes to play tricks on us." Harlow swirls her straw in her iced tea. I'm sure she is missing her Florida sun, but we make compromises when it comes to love, and that's what she did for Stone when she moved here.

"I really love this season. Crunchy leaves and pumpkin pie, you can't go wrong," I reminisce and throw a fry in my mouth. It's been a few weeks since Halloween, but autumn is still here. "How is the bambino?" I indicate to her growing belly.

She glances down and rubs her belly. "Like her father. Waking me up in the middle of the night."

I shake my head at her humor but then pause for a tick. "I was actually wondering something…"

Her shoulders slant up. "Sure."

"Uhm, maybe you and Stone need a little baby practice."

Harlow's eyes squint at me. "Uh, should I be offended?"

I laugh and realize my entry was not my strongest. "No, I'm trying to ask if maybe you and Stone could watch Bo for me?"

She's chewing on her burger and speaks with her mouth full. "Yeah, totally. What, like, for a few hours?"

I wince, and I'm wondering if this is where I face my first judgment. "No, actually…" I glance out at the lake, happy we are inside as it seems beautiful but a little windy. "Maybe overnight?" I gulp.

Harlow slowly places her burger back on her plate, now attempting to connect the dots. "As in…"

My eyes focus on the fry that I'm now toying with. "I just need a night without interruptions."

"I would love to help, you deserve a quiet night." She smooths her napkin on her lap, and her lips press before she sighs. "I don't think it's only because of you, though. Nash…" she drawls.

A long breath leaves me. "Yeah," I admit. She nods and waits patiently. "I know it's soon, but I just want to have some time alone with him. We've reconnected, and I think we owe it to ourselves to have some alone time."

She ponders for a second. "Sure," she chirps out and raises her burger to her mouth as if it's no big deal.

"Sure?" I study her, and it seems that her mood is breezy.

Harlow shrugs. "Yeah, I'm not going to be judgmental if that's what you were thinking. It's your life. As long as you feel it's a good idea, then it doesn't matter what I think."

My brows furrow. "Do you think something?"

"Hmm, you know… at first, I wasn't sure what it was, can't label this situation, but then it kind of became apparent that your lake swim might have opened a door to something between you two. Should you give yourself more time to just be yourself and alone? Maybe. But it's not my place to judge."

My face relaxes from her explanation. "Thanks. I guess it's what I needed to hear today."

Her straw makes a slurping noise. "Although, do you think you two could fall into the water again? I missed that scene, sadly." Her monotone has me concerned that she's probably serious.

It causes me to smile. "Probably not. I'm trying to draw less attention, and to be honest, that lake was a lot colder than it looks. I still freak out there are toads or something like that, too."

"I know, right? The mystery of Lake Spark's water wildlife."

I'm happy that a normal conversation overtakes us, and I'm having another day that feels promising.

We ask the waiter for the bill, and I pay since Harlow's doing me a favor. As we walk to our cars, we talk over her baby shower that is in the process of being planned.

"Okay, drop off your little gentleman when you want. Make Stone set up that portable crib thing, I want to see if he passes his nursery-construction skills." I love that she has an upbeat personality. I've heard that her beginning with Stone was not necessarily like that. We've all come a long way, I guess.

"I promise. Thanks again."

My smile doesn't seem to fade.

———

IT FEELS strange walking through the Nix family home. Of course, I've been back as an adult when Zac was alive. But visiting the house since his passing? No. I follow Nash as he checks the pool cover outside. We've added an errand to our day without Bo.

"This real estate agent is a pain in my ass." He moves a few more leaves from the blue cover as he leans over the side of the pool. "Of course it's not broken. If she just cleared a few of autumn's little sprinkles, then she would see everything is attached."

A laugh breaks out of me so fast as he stands. "Autumn's little sprinkles?"

He gives me an *oh, really* look. "What's wrong with that?"

I touch his arm "Nothing. It's cute."

Nash steps closer to tickle me. "Don't worry, I'm anything but cute."

Giggling, I do my best to shake him off. "Stop it. Wouldn't two people falling on a pool tarp break it? I mean, you and I are horrible around water."

He creates space with a wry smile and his eyes glint. "Maybe…" His thumb brushes along his jaw; I love when he does that. "As teenagers we had so many parties here," he reflects fondly.

I look around, taking in the place that was nearly my second home for so many years. "This place has a lot of good memories."

"Yeah… yeah, it does. But it's time for my parents to move on. A change of scene. Besides, they don't need a five-bedroom house."

We begin to walk to the sliding door to the kitchen, and I tuck my hands into my coat pockets. "This kitchen is great, though."

Nash swoops up my hand as we enter and slides the door shut with his free hand. "You used to bake cookies for us here."

"You guys would be on microwave duty for my popcorn intake when we would all watch movies."

"Ah yes, the family room of chilling." We stroll in no particular direction, just letting our feet lead their way out of the kitchen and down the hall.

We walk past the family den and pause for a second before we continue our journey, when Nash tugs on my arm. "Come on, we need to check upstairs too. Apparently, there's a window stuck in my parents' room."

Nothing in my mind seems to protest, it's only when we reach the top of the stairs and Nash gets to work on the agent's request and leaves me alone that a click in my mind turns on.

Sauntering down the hall, the corner of my mouth twitches when I see Zac's room. He showed it to an unaware Bo when he was born. Bo got the whole tour, and I teased that Zac's room was always so over-the-top clean as teenagers that I was always scared to even enter. It helped his study aura he believed. My fingertips tick a few times against the handle of the open door, feeling a squeeze in my heart. I will always have feelings for him in a different manner, and missing him will probably hurt forever.

Turning on my heel, I follow the carpet until I stop in front of Nash's old room. While Zac's room squeezed my heart, this room blazes it. Leaning against the doorframe, I cross my arms to soak in the scene.

It doesn't resemble the old days, when he'd had a few hockey trophies from high school on a shelf, and even though it's the same bed, it's a different duvet.

With the blinds open, the afternoon sun brightens the room, but my mind only imagines it at night when lamps were on.

I'm startled when a hand gently touches my shoulder.

"Sorry, didn't mean to scare you there," Nash states softly.

"It's okay." I can't rip my head away from the room. "Just going down memory lane, I guess."

"Right." Nash understands.

My head zips in his direction. "I mean, I was here quite a lot when I was married, and obviously, we had a few awkward family holiday dinners here over the years."

He tries to suppress his grin. "You mean, me avoiding making eye contact and barely saying a word to one another while someone asked if I could pass the green beans?"

My cheeks tighten from his perspective. "Something like that."

"I'm happy you got to lie in that bed once with me."

In an abrupt move, I offer my hand, and when our palms join, I lead us straight to the bed where we both plop on top of the mattress and stare at the ceiling from on our backs.

"Whoa, didn't think you had in you to initiate this here. I mean, how do you want me? On my back or on my knees?" He's teasing me, and I playfully hit his arm.

"Mr. Funny today," I remark. "But since Bo is with Harlow, then we don't need to rush anywhere."

Nash wiggles on the bed to get comfortable. "So true."

I sigh. "Your parents texted me that they're visiting for Thanksgiving. They want to do one last dinner here. For Christmas, they are staying south."

Nash smacks his lips together before his mouth parts open. "My mom mentioned that tiny fact."

I turn my head, and my cheek flattens against the blanket. "I'm not sure what to do."

He jostles to his side with his arms sprawled out along his body and over his head. "Me neither. My dad and I are slightly strained, and my mom, I'm not sure what sets off her emotions these days."

"They'll figure it out." My melancholy tone doesn't help the dullness of that aspect.

"Honesty is probably the way to go."

"That we've become close because you've helped me with Bo and we live together," I answer.

Nash's fingers dart out to stroke my cheek. "Except you and I actually started on this very bed."

My hand covers his, and I rest against our joined hands. "We did. Then we took a few years to let it be more. And now a few years more to be…" I have no clue how to answer.

"I'm not letting you go," he reminds me in a whisper.

"You've mentioned."

He leans in to brush his lips along mine. "Sometimes we need to untangle feelings for it to be clear."

It's as if thunder is rolling in my chest as I'm taking a chance, until sounds from my lips are the clap after lightning. "I love you, Nash, and that may be a problem."

Nash captures my bottom lip between his until he lets go, the fear not tamed inside of me after I said it. "Summer, I love you. We were idiots for not saying it back then, but maybe the words were waiting for us now, after a long road."

I bring my head to his, and our noses nuzzle. "I might have buried it for a while when life took me in a different direction, but that isn't the case anymore."

He sweeps up my hand to hold the way he does when

there is a strong reverence that takes over him. He's always been this way for his whole life. "It's always been bubbling at the surface for me."

Another kiss, and I trace my thumb over the lines of his face. "Not everyone will see it this way."

"But today nobody is looking," he whispers.

Our feelings are confirming, with no regard in my head for the consequences of what this will bring to our lives. If they are consequences at all.

———

MY ARMS ENCIRCLE Nash as he balances his focus on stirring the pot and sideways over his shoulder at the hockey game on TV between the Spinners and Dallas.

"Don't burn the house down."

"Damn it." He's not impressed, and he doesn't mean me. The hockey game must not be going in our favor.

Stepping back, I wonder if this is a lost cause. "Uhm, I'm naked and wet," I say, even though I'm in sweats.

Nope. No reaction.

"I'll get on my knees for you right here."

Still no.

I pinch his shirt and guide his attention to me. "Really?"

"What?"

My eyes grow large. "I don't mind the hockey, you know that. We can even watch after dinner. But now?" My hands splay out. "No kiddo in sight, and I believe in time management."

He grins and wraps his arms around me, pulling me flush. "Sorry. I do love the way you arranged for us to have some alone time. It kind of surprised me, but I think it's great."

I smile, feeling accomplished. "Say more."

"You're beautiful."

"More."

"I plan on making love to you."

"Hmm, might need further explanation on that one."

Nash squeezes me once. "All night. Different positions. Start with spooning and sometime during the night you'll ride me," he deadpans.

I chortle from his response. "I think I could agree to all of that." My arms snake around his neck as I almost hang off him.

His fingers dig into the sides of my thighs, and he hoists me up, setting me on the counter. "I could get used to this."

Our eyes hold as my lips press together. "I had it in my head that we could eat dinner and watch a movie like old times' sake. I guess we have plenty of opportunities in the future for that."

With purpose, Nash grazes my body as he stretches to turn off the stove knob. "Plenty," he rasps.

"One day we will walk down the street hand in hand. That will be new for us. It was never in our cards before," I point out.

Nash bends his knees and nuzzles his face into my belly. "I need to take you, Summer." He sounds desperate.

My face must confirm that I agree, as in one swift move, he has me thrown over his shoulder and carries me in the direction of the stairs.

I squeal and attempt to grip the back of his shirt. "Couldn't carry me the romantic way?" I'm flippant.

He bites into my buttocks before he slides me over his shoulder to change positions to cradle me as he walks. "Better?"

My smile nearly hurts my face. "Yeah, much better."

I'm still surprised when he manages to carry me up each step without a single sign of struggle.

When he lays me on the bed, I'm positive that I'm melting.

"Every scrap of clothing needs to come off. Not negotiable."

No hesitation from me as I begin to strip, as does he. My breath is already picking up, and we seem to turn into a frenzy of two frantic people.

The feeling of the mattress against my back doesn't cure the cold in the room. My nipples have turned into stones, and Nash's starving eyes have noticed. My body begins to warm when Nash holds his weight above me. Body warmth, right?

"You're mine, Summer." His kiss simmers against my lips. It's hard and locking me down.

My hand slips between us. I don't want any foreplay, I just want him inside of me. Gripping his shaft, I bring him to me, playing with him to wet his tip around my clit, and the moment he begins to enter me, we both groan from the pleasure.

"It seems that I'm yours," I whisper in his ear as he pumps fervently inside me.

Wrapping my thighs tighter around his waist, my eyes hood closed as I sink into the feeling of his lips skimming my shoulder. My moans grow labored, as every time he hits me to the hilt inside me, I swear I'm discovering new colors.

"I'm going to take my time and ravish you later," he murmurs against my skin. "But I'm addicted to you, and it makes me far too determined to make you come."

I chuckle under my breath. "That's in my favor, so I wholeheartedly agree."

"Well, I do have your heart, so that would make sense." I can hear the humor in his voice right before he pulls out of me and flips me to my stomach. His lips follow the trail of my spine, with his breath spreading a wildfire through my body. "I love you." His words tickle my skin in the most heavenly of ways.

He doesn't wait for me to answer before he abandons my back to kneel between my legs, and he takes the liberty to pull my waist and tilt my body until my ass is just off the bed but my upper body still down. His fingers explore my pussy, and I'm excited how he is going to take me right now.

"If you're about to fuck me until I tell you I love you again, then you better get a move on." Teasing him is a dangerous game, but I'm feeling happy today.

He slaps his palm across my ass with just the right amount of force to cause my skin to sting. "That mouth of yours is wicked today."

He takes two fingers to rub my clit, causing me to want relief from the ache between my legs. I glance over my shoulder to see him inspecting my pussy, and it doesn't make me self-conscious. Even when his fingers vacate me and I'm left hanging until Nash's finger dips inside of me, exploring my walls.

Nash has approval written all over his face, and his right hand grips the base of his shaft to give himself one stroke, then he's finding the spot he wants. Inside me.

Leaning over as he begins to thrust, his lips journey back up my spine in a tantalizing slow way, his fingers entwining in my hair to yank slightly to ensure he can amply capture my lips for a kiss.

"Tell me, Summer. Who do you belong to?" He speaks against my lips, still inside of me.

"You," I breathe out.

My answer satisfies him, and he begins to fuck me with more determination as he returns to a better position, and his hands now push my lower back down with my face squished against the pillow and his grunts sounding in the room.

Clawing the duvet, I hold on for an explosion to transpire between both of us.

And that tiny hint in my brain flashing that it might not just be in bed… I turn it off.

NASH

Throwing items into the grocery cart, I'm not exactly sure what I'm doing. First, that I'm even in the grocery store, and second, is this my avoidance tactic for the next few days? Which I'm sure I'll be called out on since I know that my mom will handle the shopping for Thanksgiving. Hell, even Summer uses the grocery store as her ruse when she needs to escape.

A coo draws my attention to Bo who is sitting the cart seat with a coat I fluffed in to prop him up.

"Bet you only want the animal crackers to gnaw on, don't you?"

No reply.

I spot the oatmeal, and even though I'm aware that Summer stockpiled a few boxes at home, it won't hurt to have one more. She might kill me. I'm here while she'll arrive home soon from work to face my parents' arrival. They insisted on making Bo their first stop before heading to their house.

"Be on your best behavior in the coming days, buddy. We

need you to distract everyone." I ruffle his hair. An indistinct sound is the response that I get. "I'll take that as an agreement."

My feet tread along like a soldier in mud, prolonging every second. I do want to see my parents. Of course, I do. Even if there is friction between my dad and me.

Seeing their grandson is the ultimate light in the past year. What I'm not eager to experience is Summer on eggshells and our nerves of indecision. We don't want them to know as much as we want them to know. Summer and I have no clue what their reaction will be, but even we know that my parents hearing of the possibility is better if it comes from us directly.

Still, how we present this is an unknown.

For a second today, I thought of visiting Zac's grave again, but it was only a millisecond, and I was watching Bo today. I don't think even Summer takes him to his dad's grave. And it's not my place to decide that.

Pulling up my phone, I see that time is not on my side. No more procrastination. I have to face everyone.

I stroke the back of my hand across Bo's cheek once. "You're about to get a lot of attention. A saving grace really. The truth is, I'm scared. Your mom thinks they will judge her, but it's probably me who will face their wrath."

But I can't break. Summer and my brother are counting on me to make it all okay.

OPENING THE FRONT DOOR, I hear the tail end of a conversation about what my mom will cook for Thanksgiving. Dropping the bag of groceries on the floor by the bottom of the stairs, I hold Nephew in my other arm. I take a few strides into the living room.

Then it happens.

My parents have smiles of happiness with a hint of sadness when their heads turn.

Summer's eyes catch with mine as she sits on the edge of the sofa arm. She must have been facing the brunt of chit-chat for who knows how long.

"There is my little bear." My mom's arms are already outstretched to take over as she stands. She looks a bit more refreshed than a few months ago. No longer frail, she must be returning to her bi-weekly trip to the salon for her nails and hair, and she's back to wearing slacks and turtlenecks with jewelry.

"Here he is." I grin and rub Bo's stomach, right before my mom snatches him out of my arms.

My father joins my mother to look down at their grandson. "Already turning into a little gentleman." Dad is just the same, stoic and wearing a polo shirt. His steely demeanor means that I've never quite figured out what he's been going through since Zac died.

My mom glances up and has a warm smile on her face. "Don't you just turn into a puddle of goo every time you see this little guy," she asks me with eyes bright.

I swipe my hand behind my neck. "Well, I'm still standing, so I guess not a puddle."

"You're just getting way too big." She's already rocking him side to side on her hip.

My eyes shift to my father who has taken a step back. His eyes have a glint in them, and as per usual, he is hard to read, but our eyes meet for a chilly recognition.

The moment is broken when Summer clears her throat. "How was the grocery store?"

"Fine. Bo loves it," I tell everyone. "Which reminds me, I should get the bag of stuff into the fridge."

"I'll help." Summer sounds way too eager, but my parents don't seem to bat a lash. They are completely in the Bo zone.

Summer and I make the quickest exit in history, and I swipe up the bag on that journey. When we're in the kitchen, I set the bag on the counter and begin to unpack. Summer helps but bubbles a laugh as she holds up a box of oatmeal.

"Don't see any items that need the fridge." Her brows rise, as she's well aware that she called me out.

"Trust me, I debated if pre-chilled wine was the way to go but decided against it. Can't have them thinking that we need a shortcut to downing some alcohol percentage."

The soft smile on Summer's face puts me at ease, and she turns to rest her back against the counter and crosses her arms. "They haven't cried yet," she mentions delicately.

On the opposite side of her, I mirror her pose. "That's good."

"Your parents only asked about the Dizzy Duck and how it's funny that I trust you to take Bo alone somewhere. More in a joking way."

My nose lifts up. "Maybe this won't be as emotional as we thought." I sound hopeful.

Summer quirks her lips out, and it's clear she doesn't quite believe me. "At some point a reminder will hit them of who is missing at Thanksgiving dinner."

I don't like hearing that realization, so I widen my eyes and survey the kitchen, deciding a snack plate for the room is in order. "You already got them drinks, right?" Avoidance of the upcoming holiday weekend is where I seem to be heading. "Maybe some cheese and crackers? I think we have olives somewhere," I jabber away as I search for crackers.

"Sure. I think they will only stay a little longer then grab dinner themselves somewhere. They must be tired from their trip."

A long sigh leaves me as I break the seal on a canister of nuts that I found in the cupboard, completely giving up on crackers. "Summer…"

She subtly touches my wrist from behind. "Nash."

"Why does it feel like the next few days are going to be hard, and it might have nothing to do with us?"

There is a brief silence. "It's the holidays. Life events or not, holidays do funny things to families."

"True." We stand in silence as I finish a plate of snacks with a bowl of nuts in the middle. I hold it up, ready to serve. "Let's get back in there."

"Yeah, I already hear Bo getting fussy."

"My parents have that effect on people." I snort a laugh.

Arriving back in the living room, my parents are sitting on the couch, praising Bo for merely blowing a bubble. "I could just eat you up, yum, yum, yum." My mother is on the overboard train, but it causes Summer to grin wryly.

"Thought we could use a snack that's not the baby," I announce and set the plate down on the coffee table.

"A good idea. Perhaps you and I can have lunch tomorrow at the Dizzy Duck?" my father suggests. "I want to see what's been done with the place since I handed over the reins." Instantly my head retreats in surprise that he wants lunch alone with me, and that humors him. "What? Thought we avoid one another the next few days?"

I don't blink, and my entire body is uncertain, but it's an olive branch that's more the size of a twig, and I will explore that. "You didn't suggest golf, so that's already a bonus." I adjust my neck. "Sure, we can meet tomorrow."

The room grows eerily quiet, and my mother notices. "Sounds like tomorrow is all set for you two. I can watch Bo, and Summer can have a bit of a rest."

"Oh, that's okay. Nash has carried a lot of the weight

around here, so I'm actually all rested up," Summer informs everyone, and she seems to notice that my mother glances sidelong at my father. They have a secret language.

"That's wonderful. Then Summer and I can grab coffee and head to the grocery store for our Thanksgiving list." My mother's smile feels sincere enough. "It will be the last holiday in the house. The realtor mentioned that there is an interested family, and they will likely put in an offer after the holiday weekend."

Somewhere inside of me, I find that disappointing. Memories swept away, but then my eyes move to Summer, and I'm reminded of them all over again, except this time new memories trickle in.

"Sounds like we all have plans for tomorrow," my father announces.

That odd chill swirls in the room again as we all exchange glances.

Summer reaches out to collect Bo. "You know, I think I'm going to get his dinner ready. I try to get him in bed by seven."

"Okay, dear." My mother smiles.

"I'll do bath time later," I say just like it's our usual day.

Lines form on my father's forehead from my readiness to help. I dial it down to the fact that me with a child is a far cry from my reckless nights as a hockey player. "Well, sounds like you both have a busy hour or two, so we'll leave you and see both of you tomorrow."

"Good night." Summer smiles.

It's a quick round of goodbyes and hugs for Summer and Bo before the air clears, and then it's back to being Summer, Bo, and me. The three of us.

The unusual emotion that flows through me causes me to wonder if I stopped breathing, which isn't even logical.

"I'm not sure what I was assuming the welcome would be. I guess I have only seen your parents a few times since the funeral." Summer lifts a shoulder. "They probably need a night to let it all sink in that they're back in Lake Spark."

I study Summer for a good long beat, and I don't want to burst her bubble as she seems to believe her words.

But I don't.

MY HANDS SPLAY OUT. "So that's the Dizzy Duck in present day," I say after the end of our tour and walk toward a table in the corner by the double windows for lunch.

There wasn't much to show since my dad was here a few months ago. Still, his attachment to this place will never vanish, and that's understandable.

"Well, now it's time to check out the menu," he tells me as he sits down, and the smile on his face isn't a lie.

Joining him by sitting across from him at the table, I'm feeling more confident that this might be a bearable lunch. "Seasonal specials, right? Maybe I can ask the chef if he can make a few of the upcoming holiday courses that will start next week after Thanksgiving. We were waiting for the decorations to come up."

"Nah, it's okay. I'm sure it will just be chicken roulade with cranberry compote."

It causes me to chuckle. "A classic, eh."

My father's mouth curves a tick into a grin. "Something like that."

He thanks the waiter for dropping off our drinks that we ordered on the way in. My brows furrow slightly on his choice of whiskey, considering it's 11:50am, but then again, I ordered an IPA beer with a solid 9.57% alcohol.

He takes a long sip then sets the glass down and slides it off to the side. "How is she?"

Here we go. I haven't even finished pouring my beer bottle into a chilled glass yet.

"Summer is doing well. Just focusing on Bo and returning to life in a healthy, natural way."

He hums a sound. "That's good. That's good," he repeats then taps his fingers on the tablecloth.

His mind is somewhere else. He's my dad, and over the years I've been qualified to understand his body language.

My eyes dip down as I debate how to break the ice, but I decide to take a hammer to it. "Just say what you've been trying to."

He smirks because he knows I've just read him like a book. "Your mom and I have different views on this situation."

"Situation?"

"The fact that Zac wanted you to move in for a little bit. Your mother would like nothing more than for you to stay with Summer. It's better than some other man stepping in."

I sigh and slouch back into my seat. "What if she didn't need a man at all? Why is everyone fixated on the idea that Summer needs a superhero?"

He snickers at me. "Because your brother had the grand idea. In truth, maybe it makes a little sense. But only for a temporary moment. You'll be leaving Lake Spark eventually, even if you already are past the six-week deadline."

"I'm staying."

My father appears taken aback, as proven by a lack of quick response and his need for another sip of whiskey. "I hope that means you'll be taking more interest in the Dizzy Duck."

"Not more than now."

"You're going to find your own place and stick around to be an uncle?" he prods for further details.

Confidence overtakes me, and I roll my shoulders back. "That's the right thing to do, and I want to. Bo is a cute little kid."

My dad's lips roll in as he contemplates. "You didn't answer the moving-out part. So, let's be clear. He's Zac's son and don't you forget that." His sharp tone has me narrowing down his thought path.

"I'm not moving out for now."

He nods subtly, only half believing my statement. "You and I haven't had the best of relationships in the past few years. It was your choice to create distance, and I can only imagine why. Now is as good a time as any to improve that, but I swear to the heavens that if you're waltzing in only to disrespect his memory, then we have no hope."

Leaning forward, I puff out a breath and rest my elbows on the table. "Cut to the chase. You don't mean Bo."

"Damn straight. Summer is vulnerable, and if you feel you need to take advantage of your late brother's wife and should something be happening that goes beyond living together, then so help me, a bridge between us just broke."

Anger swirls inside of me. Then again, what was I expecting? This isn't surprising. Eventually, he'll have to deal with it. There is no way they will break a relationship with Summer since that would entail not seeing their grandson.

Am I being selfish lately? Probably. But there is a reason. It will make sense. One day.

The waiter dropping off a breadbasket and a plate of butter shaped as a turkey doesn't seem to defuse this conversation as this stare-off is no different to the times he informed me that I should put in more effort to visit when I was playing hockey. A damn contradiction in this very moment.

"Shouldn't we just focus on tomorrow? It's Bo's first Thanksgiving and Mom's first holiday without Zac."

My father inhales a deep breath, taking a moment to calm himself. "You're right."

I have zero appetite right now. Plus, I'm wondering what Summer is facing at this very moment with my mom.

"Enjoy your lunch. It's best you and I take a breather." He nods at me, and my response is taking my knife and stabbing it straight through the butter turkey.

———

SUMMER and I stand in the shower, with the warm water spilling down our bodies.

"Really, your mom didn't bring anything up. She just seemed completely in her element with Bo, and she kept mentioning how she's happy that you're around," Summer assures me.

I grab the bottle of shampoo, even though soapsuds are already dripping down my body. "Tomorrow may not be so fun."

Summer takes the bottle from my hand and sets it back to the side. "In the end this is about Bo. We all need to put our differences aside."

"You're not the one they will be pissed off with when they find out we're together."

She snickers a sound, not impressed. "Right." Her T is tight. "I'm the damsel in distress." Summer is now annoyed because that's the last thing that she ever wants.

My fingertips touch her shoulders to calm her. "This is on me, and that's fine."

Summer wants to protest, but she stops short. "One day at a time, Nash. Now relax. Tomorrow is tomorrow." She begins to slither down my body with a mischievous smirk until she is on her knees, her playful eyes watching my facial expressions. "Let me calm your nerves."

My instinctual reflex around this woman causes my hand to smooth her hair. "Fuck, Summer."

"In my mouth? Yes, please." She plants her hands on the frame of my hips then her tongue darts out to lick my tip.

"This is how this is going to go? I get to fuck your mouth before your pussy for who knows how many hours. We'll both arrive tomorrow tired." I hiss when her mouth wraps around me.

Summer's sound is muffled because her mouth is full of my cock. My head falls back and rests against the tiled wall, taking in every lick and suck. I swear in a moment I'm going to yank her up, flip her around, spank her ass, then plunge right into her. Playful Summer in the shower is a gift from the heavens.

Her lips bind tighter around me, dragging out every pump which only brings another groan out of my mouth. I thrust into her mouth a few more times, holding her head to guide her, and when I'm getting too damn close, I pull her off.

"On your feet, Summer," I direct.

Summer's sexy face agrees with that request. Turning her until her back is flat against the wall, I raise her arms up and around my neck.

"Tight around my waist, Summer." My order is met with Summer obeying by sliding her leg up with the power of her thigh, winding me closer to her body. With one hand on the wall overhead, my other quickly swipes her pussy a few times before I plummet into her, with our moans as one.

"I needed this," I whisper into her ear as the sound of water and our bodies slapping echoes in the bathroom.

"We needed one another it seems. And not just now. Yesterday and tomorrow, too."

My teeth scrape along the base of her neck.

If only she knew…

20

SUMMER

I'm nervous. How can I not be?

Always, I knew and wanted that Zac's family would be involved in Bo's life. There was no question about that. It's just, I wasn't anticipating their other son being the one who is part of my life in a different way. The way that I'm not sure his parents would appreciate.

Waking up, I came to the realization that I'm foolish to think Nash and I can hide.

So here I am in the Nix residence kitchen on Thanksgiving Day.

"It looks delicious," I say to Gail as she cuts up the corn bread and places perfect little squares into a basket lined with a cloth napkin.

"Thank you. Always one of my favorites to bake." Her smile is wonderful to see. I'm sure this can't be easy for her, a holiday without Zac. I also feared it. That was until Nash made life a little less broken. Gail stares off into the living room. "I'm going to miss this house. So many memories." Her sight drops back to the basket. "But I can't handle another Illinois winter at my age, plus we have so many friends at the golf club in North Carolina. It makes sense. I just expect you to visit." She gives me a pointed look.

I toss the salad with a lack of effort. "Of course, we will."

"You and Bo will love it."

Right. We as in Bo and me.

We both glance to our side when we hear Bo laughing, Nash raising him up in the air as he enters the living room.

"He sure is good with him." Gail seems pleased by that. "Wasn't expecting it, to be honest. I'm happy Zac made this request. Also, that Nash seems to be staying longer. Handling his responsibilities and stepping up."

Her words draw an unexpected bewilderment from me. "You mean with Bo." My statement comes out weak, because really, I'm prying into where her mind is at.

"Sure, dear." She folds the napkin over the bread.

"I should probably go check on Bo," I mention. Mostly because I need to adjust to her comment, wondering what thoughts are brewing in her head.

Circling around the kitchen island, I mosey on over to Nash and begin to coo with Bo as I snatch his foot. "There's my little turkey. Ready for your first Thanksgiving?"

"He is. I already had him check the football schedule for today and hockey schedule for tomorrow," Nash explains as he props Bo on his hip.

Lowering my voice, I have to ask. "How is it going with your dad?"

Nash sighs. "Not so bad. We make small talk over sports."

"Good. Your mom seems fine, so perhaps dinner will go by like a breeze."

He laughs under his breath. "Miracles do happen on holidays."

The next few minutes, I leave Nash to watch Bo, and I

return to the kitchen to help. Sliding a casserole dish out of the oven, I inhale a whiff of sweet potatoes with marshmallow now melted on top. "Yum. Sweet goodness on a source of a healthy superfood."

"Alright, dear, I think we are ready to head to the table. Oh…" She snaps her fingers into the air. "Forgot to grab the highchair from the garage."

"No worries. Nash already set it up."

Gail does it again, she stalls for a millisecond before continuing her task. I don't think about it, as I have oven gloves on and am desperate to get this dish to the dining table. We both scurry back and forth, ensuring our dinner is complete.

Sitting with Nash on one side and Bo on the other, I'm not sure that I feel protected.

"Let me just get Bo sorted before we start dinner," I note to everyone at the table. Nash's dad is swirling scotch in his glass, and his mom is pouring wine and doesn't seem to mind the slight delay.

"Okay, so are we trying the green bean casserole or already giving up that Bo won't eat it?" Nash's eyes scan the array of food options, and he begins to add a few items onto Bo's plate. "We can try a little bit of the sweet potato casserole, right? Marshmallow won't kill him." He glances quickly to my side. "For sure, we're going to mush some stuffing and mashed potato."

"Yeah, exactly."

But then I see our audience sitting across the table.

"You two really have a tempo with one another," Gail says somberly, but there is a twinkle in her eye that's maybe hopeful.

I side-eye Nash and see that he's sinking into the magnitude of the next few hours. The heavy feeling that doesn't seem as though it will fade.

A secret floating around us.

"Uh, a toast before dinner, or will we just dive on in and eat this turkey big enough for twenty people?" Nash's fingers skim the wine glass in front of him.

"A toast sounds like a very good place to start." My father-in-law, Walter, holds up his glass. Following suit, I hold my glass up. "To family. For those we miss and those that are here." His voice trembles, and everyone bows their heads, probably trying to hide the crack in our hearts. "He would have wanted us to enjoy this day. For Zac."

It's a long few seconds that break when our shining light saves us; my son decided that now is the right moment to throw a little sweet potato, which causes all of our faces to soften. "He seems in agreement. Cheers," my father adds.

We all take a sip, and when dishes begin to be passed around, I'm grateful that an overload of calories will keep conversation neutral.

"You know, I think the Spinners and Pittsburg will have a good match tomorrow on the ice," Walter begins.

"Really? Maybe. The Spinners' new coach is more promising than last season, I guess." It's nice seeing Nash and his dad interact in this way.

"You must really miss it," his mother adds as she sets the bowl of salad down.

Now I have to laugh. "You know, a few people in Lake Spark have been trying to convince Nash here to become coach at Lake Spark Academy."

Everyone chuckles at that thought, except his mom who is grinning ear to ear. "That would be wonderful. You would be here permanently. Could really help with Bo."

Nash's laugh dies down. "Nah, I'll be sticking around anyway for Summer and Bo."

His innocent sentence is the match to the powder keg. I feel it in my bones because Gail and Walter give one another a look, clear as day that they've been discussing my current living situation.

Walter sets his napkin down with the air now needing a chisel to free us from this ice. "It's time for honesty."

My fear has become a reality, and I close my eyes shut tight before opening them with a tear in the corner of my eyes. Even Nash squeezing my hand under the table has no effect on my feeling of falling off a cliff, wondering if the parachute might work.

"You two are together, aren't you? Not just for Bo, either." His father's serious look confirms what should have been obvious from moment one. Gail and Walter already knew this scenario was coming.

"Yes," Nash doesn't hesitate.

Immediately, I attempt to defuse their thought. "I-i-it's not what you…" I stagger.

"Think." His father finishes my sentence.

"We happened, and I'm staying in Lake Spark." Nash is firm and far too calm for me.

Walter abruptly stands, his chair screeching, and he towers over the table as he points his finger between Nash and me. "This is completely disrespectful. I'm disappointed in both of you. Not even time to mourn and already you're both sharing a bed."

"Walter! That's enough." Gail grabs his arm.

"What the fuck did you think would happen when Zac set me up on this request?" Nash now joins everyone in this little face-off that makes me feel like a horrible person.

"I'm not trying to disrespect a memory, I promise." My

murmur to myself isn't so quiet, as everyone whips their gaze to me.

The air thickening graces us with only a moment of quiet. "Don't put this on her. Put it on me."

"Oh, I will, Nash. You're acting selfish, reckless, and most of all, basically erasing your brother." Walter is livid.

"Stop it," his mother implores. "Maybe this is a good thing. He's Bo's uncle, and I would much rather Nash step in than perhaps some other guy with no family connection. Nash won't take Bo away from us."

My rage has been unlocked, too. Standing up, my hands are clenched into fists. "I would never take him away from you. Bo's your grandson. And I'm here, you don't need to talk about me. Nor do I need someone to sweep in and help me."

"No. You just needed someone to warm your bed." His father's menacing tone causes my jaw to drop.

Gail gasps, and Nash slams his hands onto the table. "Fuck that. You know that's not true."

"We're all grieving. Maybe this is their way, Walter," Gail attempts to justify, and now it becomes clear. She wants this. Everything to stay in the family, as if it's a path of honor. In some twisted tradition, she believes Nash should be the one in my life.

Walter shakes his arm away from Gail. "Are you blind, Gail? Nash has probably been waiting, and he didn't waste any time."

"It was Zac's request!" Gail responds.

"Because Summer causes our sons to think irrationally, always has."

Nash snickers, not impressed with his dad's choice of words. "You're fucking out of line."

"You watch that tone, young man," he snipes.

"Really? Because basically calling your son's widow and the mother of your grandson a Jezebel is keeping it respectful?" He's flippant.

I've had enough, and my arms come out as though I need to be a referee. "Stop it! If you want me to feel guilty then congratulations, you have." My tears spill down my cheek, and I turn to unbuckle Bo from the seat as he fusses.

"You don't need to feel guilty," Nash reminds me.

"No?" I bring Bo to rest on my hip. "I just need to be judged, because apparently, I can't see what is so obvious. Clearly, I'm being careless with the situation."

Nash steps forward and touches my shoulder to ensure our eyes meet. "You're not doing that, either. You and I are right where we're meant to be, I promise. Love after loss, right? We just happened to find one another again."

My heart is in his hand, but the audience is throwing stones.

"Again?" his father squeaks out before grabbing his scotch glass. "Why am I not surprised. I don't even want to know the timeline of that in relation to my dead son."

Nash directs his fuming gaze to his father. "Not the timeline you think. So just please stop." His mom is shaking her head, his father emotionless gulping another sip, and I'm staring helplessly when Nash finds my eyes to keep me in a stronghold. "Don't let them bother you."

"I need to process this shitshow of a dinner," I admit.

"Don't go. We haven't even gotten a photo of Bo eating turkey." Gail seems frantic, in denial, and somehow thinks this dinner can be sewn back together.

We all look at her. "Trust me. You don't want a photo right now. So that's not happening." Nash's monotone voice brings disappointment to his mother's face. But his embrace on my eyes returns. "Don't run alone. Not when we can do it together."

Gently I shake my head. "Every dart I feared they would throw, they just did. Let Bo and me go, we'll talk later."

To my surprise, but then again Nash has always been brave, he steps forward to kiss my forehead. "We'll be okay. One day at a time."

My shoulders sink low, my body defeated, as I leave them all be, feeling as though I've destroyed their family the moment I entered their lives.

NASH

Watching Summer flee is as excruciating as facing my father who decided to cross the line on many fronts.

"What the hell was that?" I gesture with my hand to where Summer and Bo are now nowhere in sight. "Whatever your opinions, why on earth would you say all of that shit to her?"

My dad pinches the bridge of his nose and seems to have a wave of remorse. He takes a moment to gather his bearings, and then his eyes flick up to meet mine. "Okay, I was maybe a little too candid. My views are still the same."

"Summer will never want to see us again," my mom chides my dad. "She's Zac's widow and the mother of our grandson."

"Exactly. My son's widow. Last year it was Thanksgiving here with one of our sons, and now this year it's Thanksgiving with our other son." My father relays his opinion.

I shake my head as my hands clench in the air before sliding down the back of my neck, doing everything in my power not to reach for my father in pure fury. "Leave her out of this. It's me you have the problem with."

He takes hold of his scotch glass again. "Damn straight. You couldn't resist comforting her and taking advantage of the situation."

"Oh my God." I look up to the ceiling only to align my nose back down. "We're going in circles. Summer and I... we just connected, always have. We're both hurting, except... not with one another." My heart pinches because maybe to the outside world it might appear that Summer and I disregard anyone except each other.

"You know my thoughts are not far away from the truth."

"I'm going to leave you two alone," my mother says, getting up from the table. "I don't want to hear any more of this. Am I surprised you and she happened so quickly? Yes. But I'm by no means blindsided." She's disappointed with my father and me in our behavior, and she has every right to be.

We both watch her nearly march away. My chest moves visibly up and down as I count in my head to try and calm down. It's useless.

"Why the hell did you say all those things?" I grit out.

My dad crosses his arms. "Someone needed to. You need to grasp the reality of this situation. You're ignoring reality."

"What? That you pretty much just called your daughter-in-law an indecent woman?"

He licks his lips and pauses for a second. "You're right, and I'll apologize to her later."

"Damn straight you will. You don't even deserve the forgiveness that I know she will give you because she's a good person, so kind that she gave Zac everything he ever wanted."

"What does that mean?" My dad's eyes freeze on me.

Rubbing my face, I'm already exhausted from all of this. "Nothing." Only that she married and made him so unbelievably happy, even if she harbored different feelings. "You know I did everything I was supposed to. I gave up Summer, and he got her just like he wanted."

He cranes his neck and his chin tips slightly up. "Is that so? The reason you kept your distance in recent years. You couldn't overcome your pride to remain close with your brother?"

I want to respond with a denial, but… I can't, simply because it's true.

"Why don't we just get down to it and realize that Summer and Bo are not part of this. At the root, it's your disapproval of me."

My father drops onto his chair, deflated, and swipes a hand across his jaw. "You're right." Honesty is brutal, and it seems that it's about to barrel at me. "I'm angry that your brother isn't here—"

"Because the wrong son died?"

He shakes his head. "What kind of father would I be if I were to think that? So no, I don't believe that."

"Then what is the issue?"

His deep sigh in a way turns the axis of tension in the room. "I do think it's too soon for all of this to transpire. I worry that neither one of you are thinking clearly. Forgetting the repercussions if it doesn't work out or how you will fit into their lives."

Biting my lip, I hate that he's making me boil. I don't want to listen to him, even if he has points that I've chosen to ignore.

"I think you've both forgotten a few steps. It's your responsibility to ensure they're okay."

My nostrils flare, and I close my eyes tightly then open them. "What about me being okay?"

My father's lips quirk out. "Exactly. All the more reason that you and Summer are not a good idea right now. You're both trying to return to normalcy."

"Except normalcy is with her," I justify, and I'm not sure why it sounds as though I'm pleading for his understanding.

"Nash, I think we both need a breather from this conversation. I believe you're being disrespectful by you both moving on so quickly, not fully grasping the situation. That's where I stand. I need space, and I promise I'll apologize to Summer tomorrow." At least, he sounds calm and sincere. The first time in the last fifteen minutes.

Gently nodding my head, I agree that this is the best plan, too. "Fine."

Storming out, I beeline it outside, slamming the door in the process. Immediately, I see Summer finishing buckling Bo into his car seat.

"Come on, let's get out of here."

"Please," Summer agrees as she slides into the front seat.

When I'm in the car and turning on the engine, I still feel hyped up.

Summer holds up a bag. "Your mom gave us the food she still had in the kitchen." She sounds melancholy. Her shoulder lifts. "Apparently, we need an entire pumpkin pie."

I begin to back the car up, looking over my shoulder. "She's the least of our problems."

"I know. We're doing exactly what she wants. It's your father who basically thinks I'm the worst person in the world."

Focusing on the road, I remind myself that it's prime deer-crossing time. "He'll cool off. If it's any consolation, it's me he's really mad at. Thinks I'm trying to replace the missing puzzle piece in your life."

The stone-cold silence has me concerned, especially when the only sound I begin to hear is a stifling attempt not to break out in a cry.

Shit.

Of course, it's true.

"Is that what you think? I jumped in to replace him?"

In the corner of my eye, I see her gently shake her head side to side. Noticing a spot up ahead, I pull off the road, remembering the night I crashed the car with Summer in it.

The crash that happened because I broke her heart.

And here we are, in a car, with tears in her eyes all over again.

"Maybe it's true. We're in a fog and not thinking. It could just be lust or we're confusing this moment in life with reality." Summer wipes a tear away.

My entire body burns inside. I could end this pain for her in one moment, but I won't. We have to reach the destination on our own terms. "I believe we're living reality."

"Nash, everyone is thinking what we ignore. It's only been a few months and…"

Reaching over, I catch a tear descending her cheek with my thumb. "Who cares what anyone may think."

Her snicker takes me aback, and she looks at me, with the dashboard light shading her face in a light blue hue. Just as it did all those years ago. Beautiful and sad. She was the Summer I let go then. But she won't be the Summer I let go now.

"That's kind of rich, don't you think? Back then, you cared about what Zac thought so much that it destroyed us. Now it doesn't matter?"

Yet again, someone is calling me out on what I should be thinking about more.

"I-I guess…"

"Because we no longer have something blocking our way?" she highlights that fact.

Shamefully, I nod my head. "Summer, this isn't how today was supposed to go. We knew they would find out, and we were aware that it might be uneasy."

"That was a lion's den, Nash."

Finding her hand, I trap it between my palms. "You're not any of those things my dad said. He's just… dealing in his own way since Zac left us."

She exhales. "I'm aware. It's more his points about us that maybe rub me the wrong way."

"How so?"

"What is the plan? You move in? To the house that your brother bought? What about Bo? Do you raise him as your own? Or as your nephew? Can there be a difference? You and me? Are we going too fast? We never had closure, you and I. We were a car crash followed by years of silence. Maybe this is our closure."

I don't have answers. All I realize is that when I saw a moment to have her, I didn't let go. Maybe I should have given her more breathing space or just thrown her the magic sign that I've been holding onto.

"We'll figure it out."

"Don't keep saying that." She raises her voice but then glances to the back where Bo has fallen asleep. "My world is spinning," she whispers. "I'm in a car with you, and it doesn't feel like last time. I see it in your eyes. You won't let go this time."

"I won't," I promise.

Her lip trembles while she wipes away another tear with

the back of her hand. "Why do we keep ending up in these places?" She attempts to smile. "A car or that ridiculous dock."

Letting go of her hand, I choose to hook my finger under her chin to guide her gaze to me. "Want some good news?"

"Yes."

"The cookies at the Dizzy Duck are now shaped as snowmen."

It causes her to giggle and cry at the same time. "That is good news."

Leaning down, I capture her mouth for a kiss, not caring about the salty tears. I just need to ease her. My heart wants to wrap around her and lock her in.

It's so painfully obvious to me right now.

My brother left her in pieces when she became a widow, and now I'm bringing her to pieces because of confusion of what is right. That's two times broken in a short time. It makes sense why this is so difficult for her.

It should be for me too.

But I'm too strong and greedy.

The moment our lips part, she places a soft kiss inside my palm. "Tomorrow, I think I'm going to see my brother since he finally unpacked all of his moving boxes in his new house."

"Okay, we can do that."

She shakes her head. "No. I want to go alone. I need a little breathing space."

My stomach drops with fear that she's running away with regrets, but at the same time, she needs to get perspective. She deserves that. "Sure, are you taking Bo with?"

"If it's okay, I'll leave him with you. Your mom wanted to spend time with him."

Her kindness is in full swing. That's just Summer. Her heart is soft for others and hesitant around only me.

"You know I love you, right?" I remind her.

"I do, because I love you too. I'm just a bit of a wired mess now."

I kiss her again on her mouth, eager to shake her until she believes that everything will be alright.

But true love is when you let someone find their path to you on their own terms.

Which is what I will give to her.

SUMMER

How did I end up here?

In the Dizzy Duck Inn reception on the day after Thanksgiving, bright and early at 9am. Nothing is going according to plan today. Then again, it hasn't been for months.

Staring down at the pile of papers, I can't believe I forgot to sign off on the invoices that need to be paid by Monday. My mind has been muddled lately to say the least.

Staring at my name on the paper, I still sometimes wonder how a name could inflict so much emotion. I'm carrying the last name that has changed my life.

Sliding the papers into a yellow envelope, I write a quick note so Holden knows the contents. Now I can get on my way and drive to my brother's. My plan is to stay there until late afternoon.

Sighing, I turn to leave the lobby, but I hear someone call my name.

My eyes search and find an older lady who is smiling brightly at me. "Mrs. Nix?"

I point to myself. "Me?" She nods, and I step forward. "Is

it my mother-in-law that you're after?" After all, what does this old lady want with me?

Her smile remains. "No, dear, you. You live in my house now."

"Oh. You must be Mrs. Grace?" I never met her, but I heard about the friendly lady.

"Yes. I'm staying here while I'm in town to see my granddaughter. I do hope that you're enjoying my old house."

"What's not to love."

Her eyes bow for a second. "I'm sorry about your husband."

My lips purse out. "Thank you. "

"He was a special man. You know, when he heard I might sell, he first came to me almost two years ago, asking if I would sell early. I thought it was the most heartbreaking thing."

My head perks to the side. "How so?"

"He told me how he was dying and wanted to ensure that you would have the house and everything you would need."

"W-what?" It makes no sense. He only found out he was terminal a month before Bo was born. Everything happened so quickly. "It can't be. He was sick but not that sick then."

Confusion paints onto her face. "Huh. I clearly remember him telling me how he didn't have much time. He pleaded with me to sell because he thought it would be a house that you would want. I wasn't quite ready, even though he pulled on my heartstrings."

"But I only moved in much later."

She shrugs. "Well, I only decided later."

"Are you sure you have the timing right?" It simply can't be. Zac wouldn't have kept that from me.

Mrs. Grace seems to grasp that she's sharing new information with me, and she gently touches my shoulder. "Forget what I said. I'm just happy you live in my old house. It's a perfect little place."

I nod with an attempted closed-mouth smile. "Uhm, I need to be somewhere, but it was lovely meeting you." Swallowing, I do my best to digest her information. "Have a lovely holiday weekend."

"You too, dear."

Fleeing, I find myself behind the wheel of my car, paused and wondering what the hell.

"I've made sure that you have everything that you'll need, I promise."

Shaking my head, I'm even more happy now to get the fuck out of Lake Spark.

―――――

WANDERING through Keats's home to the kitchen, it's clear this restored old house is far too big for him. Despite the farmhouse kitchen that brings a bit of lightness, this place screams bachelor pad, down to his tray of whiskey tumblers and crystal decanter near a restored fireplace.

"Juice or water? I actually went to the grocery store this morning," he informs me as he disappears behind his fridge door.

Sitting at the island, I twiddle my thumbs as I tell him a water.

He reappears with a bottle for me. "I'm happy you came, though without my nephew, but still a relief that you feel this place is a refuge. I just wish it was under better circumstances."

My lips twist as I play with the cap of the water bottle. "I wanted some air to clear my head, and since you said you wanted to work yesterday and let me enjoy time alone with the Nix family, then I have no choice but to drive here. And trust me, I didn't enjoy the time alone."

Keats reaches out to soothe my arm with his hand. "I'm sorry. I wish things were better. They didn't take it well that you and Nash are something, did they?"

"His father, absolutely not. Gail seemed okay. She wants to keep me in the family, even if that means switching sons. I'm getting confused if I've ruined their family or if they ruined my life. But after unraveling it all, I'm well aware that they didn't destroy my life and they probably didn't mean their words."

"Nah, they don't hate you or anything. They're just sensitive considering the last year. But to be honest, the parents are not bothering you. It's something else. Or rather someone."

Clawing my hair with my fingers, I growl a sound of frustration. "I love him, but I fear I've been blinded." My hands slide down to rub the back of my neck. "Everything is spinning so fast that I'm not sure I'm looking the right way," I admit. The clouded judgment isn't just a theory, I'm now an example of it.

"Summer, I was convinced that's what you and Nash are. But you smile around him, seem more yourself. It's more a question of if you're truly ready to move on."

Licking my lips, the question in my head confronts me again. "That's when the guilt cycle begins to turn. I've never really moved on from Nash, just tucked him away. It's a horrible thing to say out loud because I had a husband, but I loved him too, just in an altered way. Not many people would realize that, nor am I going to correct them. Zac wanted a wife, and he got one, so I won't let the world know that it was anything different."

"You never explained it fully, but you're my kid sister, and it was always my sixth sense."

"The thing is… to everyone it must appear that Nash is sliding right in where his brother left off, but I don't see any other way. It's a wall about what the future may look like. I'm just stuck in a moment."

Keats tips his head in the direction of the couch. "Come on. This conversation deserves a more relaxed setting."

I half smile in agreement and hop off the stool. Walking to the living room, I glance out the window to see the gray sky and notice the neighbor's house. "It's empty. Your new neighbor hasn't moved in yet?"

"Why? Want to move closer to me? You know I would love it."

"Ha, ha. You've offered many times for Bo and me to move in here for a bit, but we're staying in Lake Spark."

My brother flops onto the sofa. "The neighbor better move in soon, otherwise I swear a family of raccoons might take up occupancy. Now back to you, and no more small talk." He narrows his eyes at me.

I salute him that I shall listen. "The wall, right?" I check to remember where we left off, and he nods to confirm. "I don't think I see any other paths with Nash, but responsible me reminds myself that we are skipping a lot of steps."

"Well… he does live with you."

I roll my eyes. "Which feels like that might be a strange story, too. I think I just need to hear it one more time from someone that I'm allowed to be happy, and it just so happens to be with Nash."

"The guy annoys the shit out of me, but he loves you. If he makes you happy then it's okay."

"Maybe I should slow us down, you know? Suddenly, Bo has more than an uncle in the picture. Nash is so much beyond. We have to tread carefully."

Keats stares at me blankly. "Bo chews on his foot. He is fine."

I crack a smile at his comment. "As true as that is, I wouldn't want to do anything that will affect him. Nash is… great with him. None of us expected that. Maybe I didn't want that. I was counting on him leaving after six weeks, yet he didn't leave at all."

"Sounds to me that you get to have everything you wanted. A friendship and a son. And now the guy who I'm fairly positive you wanted all along. Now you just need to come to terms with it."

My eyes grow as I sigh. "You're supposed to be solving this situation for me. That's kind of crazy too. Your romantic life needs improvement." I pinch his arm.

"We're focusing on you today," my brother deadpans.

"I'm kind of surprised how calm you are. Considering my life is imploding, I thought for sure you would go brother bear on me."

"Meh, as much as I want to punch a few people, it's a holiday weekend. I'm being considerate. Besides, Nash hasn't *actually* done anything wrong. It's you and what's inside of your head that's the problem. The pin will drop any moment, I feel it."

I have to smirk at his optimism. "Did you really just have a few drinks with friends last night after work? Are you sure they didn't slip anything into your food?" I joke.

"Funny." He slides his eyes to the side then back to me. "Take the afternoon to breathe and lightning will come. Now don't fucking ponder any more right now, I want to take you for lunch or at least try this coffee place in town. I would say it's part of my marketing plan to get you to move here, but I think you would much rather still refresh and start your life anew in Lake Spark."

My brother cares so much, and it makes the corners of my mouth hitch. "You're probably right. In fact, I know you're right. Just need a little more time to clear my head."

Keats stands up and offers me his hand. "Coffee it is then."

Chipping the brick away. It takes time. I'm not there yet, but the brick wall is getting smaller.

———

ARRIVING BACK TO MY HOUSE, I see the lights on upstairs which tells me that Nash is home and probably getting Bo to bed. I was expecting that. I just wasn't expecting Walter to be waiting in his car on the street.

This was bound to happen at some point, but still, I slide out of my seat with a little dread. He exits his car and walks toward me. Closing my door, I take a few steps to meet him halfway.

"Summer."

"That's me." I avoid looking at him and examine the area instead. The outside lights are enough for us to read one another.

He clears his throat. "I owe you an apology. A big one."

My shoulders sag, and my mouth quirks out. "I think you also said what you think."

"Maybe so, but I could have worded it better, and I was out of line. It's just hard to figure this all out. They're both my sons and very different in all ways. Except they share one thing in common, and that's... you."

My gaze snaps in his direction, and he must sense that he caught me off guard. "I believe you realize that, too."

Crossing my arms around my body, I inhale a long breath

only to let it fall out. "I don't want you to think that I'm a horr—"

He holds his palm up in protest. "I don't, so no need to say it."

"How long have you been waiting?"

"Nash was with Gail all afternoon, and he mentioned you would be back later. I arrived here and he was already upstairs. He hasn't realized that I'm here."

I chortle a laugh. "Maybe that's for the best. I want to remain on good terms with my neighbors."

Walter seems to find that amusing. "Probably a good idea."

A long pause lingers around us.

"Again, I'm sorry. I might not be forgotten, but I just wanted to let you know that I'm sorry."

"Consider it forgotten and move on." My personal crime, giving forgiveness so easily. I do it a lot. Especially with men from this family.

"You make it too easy on us. You know if you just held your ground a little more then maybe it will be easier to move forward."

Now I laugh to myself. "I think I'm offended by that comment but to hell with it. We can sweep the last forty-eight hours away and just… tomorrow, you and Gail can spend more time with Bo before you head back."

He nods. "Thank you." He begins to leave, but a thought comes to me.

"Uhm, an unusual question. It's just the timeline in my head is blurry, and things happened so quick when we realized that Zac wasn't going to get better. Only two months and then he was gone. Right, two months?" Not a year.

Nash's dad scratches his cheek. "Yeah, Summer. Your memory serves you well."

"A silly question, I'm sorry. Just… have a good night."

I'm not sure if the air is eerie or hopeful or just plain strange. At least I got an apology, and it did feel as though he felt remorse. I kind of have enough issues as it is to let it bubble in my head.

Settling back home, I set my coat and purse by the door, take my shoes off, and go upstairs. When I reach the top of the stairs, I can already see that Nash is tiptoeing out of Bo's room, clearly having just put Bo down.

"Hey," he whispers.

"Hi. I guess I just missed it."

Nash steps to the side. "Have a look."

I walk on the balls of my feet to keep quiet and then peek through the half-open door to hear a little snore. My little heart, forever he will be.

Warmth of a hand on my shoulder causes my head to turn to Nash. "A good day?"

"He was fine. You?"

"I'm tired."

Nash scoops up my hand to guide me to my bedroom, or is it our bedroom? What a muddle of logistics. "Want me to leave you be?" he checks in, because it seems he's reading my thoughts.

"Tomorrow we'll talk. For now, let's go to sleep. Hold me under the covers, Nash. That's what I need," I coo, wanting to say nothing, and instead, comfort is what I want now.

He nods in understanding, and as he tows me toward the room, I glance over my shoulder to the room of white noise and nightlights then back to Nash.

"Don't worry, Summer. I've made sure that you have everything that you'll need, I promise."

It floats in my head, pushing me to the finishing line.

NASH

Waking, I feel Summer sitting on the edge of the bed. She's reaching behind to fasten her bra, and I drag my body up to sitting to help her. It flashes in my head, how I always used to do this.

Then and now.

"Here," I say as I close the hook and inhale the mango scent from her shower gel. She fell asleep quickly last night after causing me to burst out laughing when she said my father apologized, until I realized she wasn't joking. I was relieved, as that just meant one less thing to worry about. Still, Summer seemed worn out, and I just followed her cues and let her close her eyes in my arms. Whatever is on her mind or mine, it didn't seem to ruin our deep sleep. "Morning."

Summer barely glances over her shoulder with a look of appreciation then swipes the sweater that she had set on the bed. "Good morning. Didn't mean to wake you, thought you could sleep in."

Rubbing my eyes, I feel the haze of sleep fade away. "It's okay. I would rather we talk and spend the day together."

That remark earns me a smirk. "If you don't mind, I'm just going to spend the day with Bo. I want to make up for yesterday not being here, and Harlow suggested we meet for coffee."

She's avoiding me. It isn't rocket science.

"Sure. Want me to get Bo dressed?"

Summer is already standing and zipping up her jeans. "It's okay, he's just in his crib playing around with his stuffed monkey."

"That little dude can scare away all of his bad dreams."

Her closed-mouth smile feels promising. "Doesn't change the fact it's a freaky little thing."

She quickly leans down to give me a peck on the lips. "We can meet later."

I grab her wrist before she can escape. "Are you avoiding me? Is that what this is?"

Her lips press together. "Maybe. I just want a little more time to clear my head, you know? Plus, you probably need it too."

Reluctantly letting her wrist free, I don't debate her. "Okay."

The good news as she walks out the door is that she doesn't seem to be as down as yesterday, but the bad news is that she still needs time.

My eyes drift to the drawer where somehow, I've occupied with my things in such a short period. Items in a drawer that hide a solution she doesn't realize.

Shaking my head, I throw the sheet hanging around my waist off. I'll head to the ice rink to wear off some tension. It's been a week since the Dizzy Duck management meeting on the ice. Today, I just want to skate alone.

———

AN HOUR LATER, I'm on the ice, but I don't get my wish to be alone.

"Seriously, I thought Lori was going to throw her phone at me. She flipped out, and Lexi just watched like it was some reality show," Holden explains as he slowly skates next to me.

I have to laugh. "Who the fuck tells their teenager that they're in charge of taking the group of friends to the movie theater and that they are staying to chaperone? If I were her, I would have thrown a lot more. Let them be and make sure they're home by eleven."

We pass the puck gently between us with our sticks, well aware that there are a few other people on the ice, including a few kids. "Trust me, when you're a dad, you'll understand the protective overboard nature." Holden immediately pauses when he realizes his choice of words. To be honest, I don't even know how to interpret it. "I mean, it's not that you're not a da— You're an uncle, but you're…" He winces, as he must feel as though he is sinking into a melting pile of ice.

"It's fine. I'm not even sure how to label this. Of course, I'm protective of Bo, I just need to figure out how to navigate the role without replacing a piece, you know? It's one of the reasons why Summer has been freaking out lately. Not helped by my dad being a complete jackass."

"That bad, huh?"

My head cocks to the side slightly, but I don't need much time to evaluate. "A shitshow, to be honest. Summer went to visit her brother yesterday to escape. Now, we haven't really spoken since the other day." I lift the puck with my stick and begin to toss it in the air. "It doesn't seem to be bad for me, but I'm not sure."

"It will come around." Holden gently touches my arm to

prevent me from skating forward. "And hey, about the parent thing. Maybe slightly different, but Lexi treats my kids as her own. The parenting dynamic comes in different shapes but something feels as though it isn't the greatest issue."

I begin to skate in a circle around him. "It's not. For fleeting moments, I remind myself that I'm a greedy asshole and should probably give Summer space, nor should I have led us down this path. I mean, what kind of brother am I? Stealing his wife after he's barely been laid to rest. But then… everything indicates that I'm right where I should be. I'm already confident about that. I've just been waiting for Summer to catch up. I don't want her with me for the wrong reasons. But my patience sometimes runs thin."

"What's the next step?"

"She wants to talk tonight. That's a good thing, except… I might have something to make everything go away…" Because I've been hiding something from her all along.

Holden seems puzzled. "Be honest with her. Don't do something stupid. I learned my lesson the hard way." We skate toward the exit, and Holden groans. "Shit. Principal Johnson. How can I not escape that woman? Even when my kids are well behaved. She must be visiting her daughter who is back from college."

I glance to my side. "You have horrible luck."

Then he gets a devious look on his face. "Nah, I think it will change. I'm saying hi then mentioning that you're sticking around and that you two should chat." He winks at me before skating off, not giving me a chance to protest.

I smile tightly when Principal Johnson approaches the exit of the ice, ready to pounce with her over-the-top grimace. "What a lovely surprise. I've mentioned that Lake Spark Academy is…"

What the hell, I have some time to kill. I might as well humor everyone for the next thirty minutes.

———

SOME WOULD SAY the holiday lights at night on Main Street and the shop windows lit up are magical. Except seeing Summer pacing back and forth on the corner of the street causes my heart to clasp around a speck of fear, and I dip my fingers into my pocket to feel the crinkle of glossy paper.

She asked me to meet her here since Bo is with Harlow and Stone. Summer was on a walk then sounded adamant that I come to meet her here. The house is too confronting, perhaps, and the dock has been overused for our life confrontations.

Summer's eyes draw up from the ground to face me as she shakes out her hands. "The thing is, Nash." Oh, okay, she's going straight into this. "I'm not some toy that's been tossed around between you and your brother. Sometimes it feels that way, and I'm not that woman. You are every red flag that I've been warned about. You could run away at the first hint of a challenge. Or realize you're confused too in a time of mourning." Her impassioned words are causing her breath to stagger, and her body is anything but calm.

"Summer, are you sure you want to talk about this right now?" As I move forward, she takes a step back, clearly adamant that we will continue this conversation in public.

"Yes. I need to get this out now. For the last few weeks, I've been beating myself up about how life is transpiring, except… it's with you, and that's a missing piece that I've been waiting for." Her face shifts, and I see the blaze in her eyes. "You know, your brother lied to me, to all of us. He knew he wasn't going to make it long before we did. I just discovered that little fact, but it makes sense now. It's as though he was playing a game of chess." There is anger in her voice.

My jaw flexes side to side from her revelation as dots begin to connect in my head. "What do you mean?"

"You and I?" She throws her arms up in the air, and the glint of her treasure necklace catches the light just right as she begins to walk away. "This shouldn't be happening, Nash," she nearly yells.

Following her, I grab her arm to ensure she faces me again. "You know that's not true."

I'm still fighting for her it seems. It's as though I'm staring at a wall, debating if there is a crack or not.

A tear falls down her cheek. "Which is exactly why… you're right." The certainty of her words catches me by surprise, with a swoosh of air wrapping around me. She isn't fighting. "I want you. I want this. No more running. No hiding. I won't feel guilty, and I'm allowed to have this, us," Summer lists, overwhelmed with emotion.

Instantly, I step closer to her and touch her shoulders, ready to pull her close. I couldn't care less that probably half the street has heard us or that we have an audience.

My own breath is heavy as I'm melting with Summer. "I've been waiting for you to figure it out."

"How so?"

I squeeze my eyes shut then open. "We've returned to one another because of us. The situation gave us that opportunity, but it's our feelings that have us standing here together, wanting it all." I gesture to the street, and I swear Holden and Lexi are lurking across the street watching this confrontation between Summer and me. "I've been lying to you."

Summer's breath catches and concern floods her face. "What do y-you mean?" she stammers.

"The thing is, I came back to Lake Spark, and the moment I saw the opportunity to make you mine again, I selfishly took it. Then, I had a sign that it was okay. I just… didn't tell you. I wanted you to find your way to me because *you* wanted me. Not because you got a nudge."

Summer glances to the side then back to me, her tongue sweeping across her bottom lip. "I think we got that as we lived together. It's like he was plotting for a while." She nervously laughs as if it's a joke.

But my stomach drops because it is no joke.

Shoving my hands in my pocket, I debate what is the right thing to say right now. "I love you, and we're right where we should be. You're with me on this, right? We're together, and you're comfortable that we're happening and have a future for the right reasons?"

She nods, with honesty written all over her face.

"Plotting isn't a far stretch. We may never have told my brother about us, but he couldn't have been blind, and he left this for me to find…" Sighing, I take the photo from my pocket and hand it to her.

Summer's gaze drives down to the photo to see the three of us from all those years ago, then she flips it over. It feels as though I'm reading it with her, and both of our minds catch up with our hearts. Her eyes strike up to meet mine, and we share a similar look. An inescapable emotion, and our sight drops again to the back of the photo.

"It seems we all knew that you and I would end up where we always should have been," I state softly.

Maybe it's the doodle he drew of her necklace or maybe it's simply his writing. But the words vanish all worries because her mouth quivers yet forms a soft smile as she reads aloud.

"'For someone who loves treasure, I ensured she got her crown jewel. I was her first husband, but you'll be her last.'"

She looks up. "And that's why he told me... 'Don't worry, Summer, I've made sure that you'll have everything you need, I promise.'"

24

SUMMER

Nash lays me down on the bed, his body over me and his eyes intent on staying locked with mine. This whole evening is a shock but only a soft one. Underneath everything, we always knew that the cards were set up. Just now, we've accepted it.

His brown eyes have a glint that's new, a reflection that's changed. The feeling of his stubbled jaw brushing along the line of my face brings a smile to my face.

"I love you." His words drag along my skin before his teeth scrape my bottom lip.

My body bucks up and shapes to his form. I need him inside me to the hilt, our breaths mingling and our bodies never untying tonight.

I chase his mouth and capture him for a kiss. A deep kiss that lingers and plays, before our eyes follow patterns together. "I love you," I whisper.

Nash takes a moment to let me go and lifts his shirt up. He leans down to help me with my own, but I beat him to it, but I do allow him to slide my jeans off and every scrap of clothing that remains on my body. I'm not sure why but the sound of a buckle coming undone only heightens my desire that's building far more quickly than we might like. But we have all night to do this over and over again.

I do my best to rub against Nash for friction because I'm becoming unhinged and can't lie still. He knows it and grins right before his tongue swirls around my nipple, with his hand skimming and leading my arm up against the mattress over my head.

A moan falls off my tongue, and the sensation of the tip of his cock sliding between my thighs lands exactly where I want him to, on my clit, which only causes more desperation.

"Nash, please."

He doesn't use words to respond, instead shifting his body, and he trails his lips down my body until he stops right above my pubic bone where his nose nuzzles side to side to make this moment an agonizing wait.

"We have all the time in the world, Summer." His tongue arrows out to lick an indistinct pattern against my skin.

Every pulsing sensation that I could possibly have swims in waves through my body. "Yet, you couldn't get me up here fast enough."

He chuckles with that deep velvety tone. "Forgive me for wanting a moment to cherish this body that is mine."

"Nash," I gasp. "Then mark me inside."

That remark only earns me his chuckle, turning to a devilish smirk, his finger skating between my slit for a swipe. It should be a crime when the pad of his finger taps my clit for a few beats. My body is on fire, and I do my best to tilt my body to guide his cock to enter me.

But then he kisses my neck as he leads his cock straight to where I want it. The groan we share when I feel him fill me up still doesn't bring even the slightest release to the ache between my legs that keeps building. Not even after a few thrusts and more moments of moving together.

When he is as deep as he can get, with nowhere to go, we pause. I should be screaming, but I don't mind because our eyes meet for acknowledgment that everything will be okay. The spark between us remains as always, it can't fade.

"Seems we get forever." It barely escapes my lips, but everything about those words warms my heart. I'll photograph the look on Nash's face in my head and cherish it forever. He agrees and is as happy as I am.

His grin begins to form "Well... I don't plan on making this moment last forever. I kind of need to fill you up, and I'm nearly about to explode."

Naturally, I clench harder around his cock and tighten my legs around his waist, and I hiss. "Tsk, tsk, someone was adamant that we could even go slow right now. What happened to my captor?"

Teasing him only causes Nash to pump inside me harder and faster again. "He's reminding your soul that I'm the only guy you'll ever be sharing a bed with."

It's no longer a prospect which is why we meet for a bruising kiss that isn't sensual but good all the same, and I smile when our lips part.

We both race toward complete bliss in bed.

But for our life too.

HE'S the perfect pillow and his fingers the perfect feather on my back. Nash and I haven't left the bed, even though the sun came up about an hour ago.

"You're okay with me staying here or would you eventually want to move?"

I roll my eyes again. "Yes. I'm fine with you staying here on a non-temporary basis, and for now we don't need to think about other houses. My brain can only process cleaning up toys in the living room and searching for that damn proboscis monkey that keeps getting lost." The feeling of his chest vibrating with a rumble of a laugh is a calming moment.

We've been talking about a few things since we woke up. A few topics Nash keeps bringing up on repeat; I guess he needs certainty of what I meant last night. Everything still holds true. I'm comfortable and certain.

"I kind of forgot to tell you one more thing," Nash tells me.

My head perks up from that sentence. It's been a lot of life changes in the last twenty-four hours. "Oh, uhm…"

The fear that my face must portray only cracks him up, and his hand soothes my arm. "Relax. Just wanted to prove to you that I won't run away nor be a pain in your ass and bother you at work every day—although, I am ten percent owner—and I'll keep myself busy beyond baby talk and toddler-proofing."

"How are you going to do that?" I'm clueless.

His jaw moves side to side, and he winces. "I kind of…"

"What?"

"Agreed to help coach the hockey team at Lake Spark Academy."

My body halts as I let that sentence melt into my brain. It's like a ding in my head, and my laugh is beyond bursting, it's a volcano. My laugh is so powerful that it causes Nash to be kind of annoyed. "Really? Like, *really* really?" I flop to my back, feeling tears forming because my stomach is hurting from my laughter.

"Yeah, really." He moves to his side and looks down at me. "I can do it," he protests.

"Sure you can." I pat his arm because he's adorable.

"Calm it down, will ya?"

I swallow my last chuckle. "You're right. My apologies. I do think you will be good at it. Just the full circle of life is hitting us in one big wave. Except this one? My hockey guy returns to the birthplace of his wildness to try and tame teenagers. This is going to be… a little epic."

"Ha, ha." He tickles me and now my face hurts from smiling.

But then the room calms, and it's a heavy silence.

"Uh, Summer…" He swipes his thumb across his morning stubble.

A ting hits me, but I stay poised. "Bo."

He nods once.

I reach up to comb my fingers through his hair. "You'll be as good a father to him… but we'll always remind him that you're his uncle."

Fondness floods his face. He doesn't need to say any words, we're both on the same line when it comes to that. Deception has no part when you're living in honesty and memory.

It takes a moment for us to snap out of our serious moment, but I know just how. My finger lands on Nash's mouth to shush him. "No marriage talk now, mister."

Because he'll bring it up again.

He bites my finger playfully. "Fine."

I hum that I'm in a peaceful state. Nothing is heavy around my heart anymore.

As flawless as waking up like this is, we also have to hustle our way out of bed and get a move on. I begin to wiggle, and Nash takes it as our sign.

"How could we forget that we have a little guy to pick up?" he says as we both leave the warm sheets.

"We didn't forget. We just chose to discuss important matters… and perhaps, steal a few extra minutes of sleep." I ramble that sentence out because it's completely true.

Nash is already walking to the bathroom with a grin.

My eyes wander the room, and a shiver hits me that causes me to feel cold then instantly warm, and my lips quirk from that, and I step comfortably forward in the direction of the bathroom, to a door.

Doors open.

———

"THANK YOU AGAIN. I know it was only supposed to be a few hours, and then, well, that plan changed and—"

Harlow calms me by sputtering a laugh, with her hand on her belly, as we sit in the lobby of the Dizzy Duck Inn. "Oh, honey, I never thought you would be gone for only a few hours." She glances down to Bo in his stroller. "Mommy was being silly, wasn't she." Her baby voice doesn't need any improvement; she's going to nail the mom thing. "Then when Holden and Lexi texted about the fireworks on Main Street between your mommy and uncle, then you and I just got cozy for the night, didn't we?"

My son giggles and grabs his feet in the air. He doesn't seem to have missed me.

"I guess it was obvious."

"Well, I mean, all of us are already aware, it's just you two kind of kept it under the radar, so we were never sure how to act. Are you openly together so we can all calm down?"

I smile and stare at my son. "All good on the public front."

Harlow pretends to wipe her forehead. "Phew. Lexi was

planting mistletoe all around the hotel. Little booby traps so we could see you two attempt not to kiss when you really want to kiss, but then you do kiss and question it, only to kiss again," she babbles, and it's her romantic heart at work.

"It's fine. Make a map for where I can find the hanging plant," I gladly declare.

The sound of two men laughing brings my gaze to my right. Stone and Nash are joining us, and it seems they must have been discussing anything but the running of the Dizzy Duck Inn.

"Ready to nosh on some brunch while my parents debate a Virgin Bloody Mary or not?"

I snort a laugh and stand. "That's not even in question."

Next to Nash where I should be, his elbow runs along my arm as he slips on the diaper bag and makes a funny face at Bo.

"Have fun. The croissants with local jam never fail at our fine establishment," Stone jokingly reflects.

"Yeah, it's the broken coffee machine that's shit," Nash points out.

Shaking my head, it's nice to be lighthearted today. "No more Dizzy Duck critique." I begin to push the stroller.

It's a quick round of goodbyes, then Nash and I make our way to the dining room.

When we enter, we spot his parents in the corner. It's their last day here before they head back south. Their demeanor is different to a few days ago, no longer tense but still resigned.

They too will find harmony; maybe not today but soon, I'm sure.

Nash and I are thinking clearly.

We have a future.

No sin is involved because there never was to begin with.

Maybe it's the flick in our eyes that meet his parents' or

the fact that we know we have Harlow, Stone, Holden, and Lexi as unexpected spies who are not so casually sipping on mimosas at the bar, pretending not to watch.

Everything is hopeful.

Which is why Nash and I look to one another with a smile then interlace our fingers to hold hands.

Because we're together.

EPILOGUE: SUMMER

SIX MONTHS LATER

"Are you sure you're going to be fine? I mean, that big shot lawyer guy from Colorado is staying this weekend," I explain as Stone and Holden stand in front of the reception desk. They stare at me, unfazed, with their arms crossed.

In fact, Stone is casually drinking from his to-go cup of coffee. "Oh, whatever will we do if a fire starts and the Lake Spark fire department is busy saving a deer somewhere," he deadpans. He probably thinks I'm being ridiculous.

My head cocks to the side from his demeanor.

"Go. Go on your much-deserved day off," Holden assures me.

I nearly snort a laugh. "Seeing my brother isn't exactly a holiday. There's a fifty-fifty chance that Nash and Keats will get along."

Holden quirks his lips and thinks to himself for a second. "I think they'll be fine. You have a kid to distract them."

A proud smile hits me. "Yeah, Bo is the best ever, isn't he?"

"I mean, let's not go overboard. My little guy is going to be the best little superhero in the making," Stone highlights. He's glowing like a proud father does.

Stuart clears his throat; I always forget when he's around. Peeking around Stone and Holden, I see Stuart staring up from the tablet at the desk. "Could you do one more thing for me before you go?" He rolls his shoulder back and seems afraid to ask.

Poor kid, Stone still makes him nervous. "Sure," I reply, my smile still intact.

"On the dock, there seems to be a guest who wants to complain about the rowboat."

I grumble to myself. "Really?" I answer dryly. "That's what I have to deal with before I go?"

"We would offer to step in, but we have places to go and people to see. Enjoy your free day, Summer," Holden states as he and Stone propel themselves from the desk. Stone gives me a little nod and smiles as they walk away.

"Cookie?" Stuart's upbeat tone is back as he holds up the basket of welcome cookies.

My brows knit together. "What shape?"

His eyes dip down, and he examines the basket. "Uh, we're back to the traditional chocolate chip. Oh, there is this odd-shaped one."

My hand finds my hip that tips out. "Odd-shaped one? We are serving our guests deformed cookies?"

Stuart shrugs, and I'm quick to snap the cookie from the basket, completely unenthused. I look at the cookie then do a double take. My head lolls softly to the side. Huh? Is this…

"I think the dock issue is waiting," Stuart reminds me, and now I realize that he has been setting me up.

The cookie I'm holding between my two fingers isn't an odd shape.

It's a treasure chest with icing.

My frustration with work vanishes. "Thanks. I better get a move on."

The pace of my walk is nearly a skip through the Dizzy Duck until I stop at the door to the back patio. My hand stills on the handle as a rush of blood pumps through my body. Slowly opening the door, I'm greeted with the vision that I'll never get bored of.

Nash is standing on the dock, holding my son's raised hands, his nephew. Bo is strong but can only walk with our help. Any day now that will change.

I make my way to them, wrapping my arms around my body to keep me warm from the gentle breeze, and the moment my feet touch the dock, I'm aware that I won't be leaving as the same woman.

Holding up the cookie, I grin, because Nash has a suave look that shows satisfaction to his plans. "Nice cookie request." Ceremoniously, I take a bite.

His smirk knocks every nerve inside my body to red alert that Nash will make me happy. "Beats those damn ghost shapes," he replies.

I step closer, my eyes meeting his for a few ticks before I lean down and offer Bo the remainder of the cookie.

Nash lets his hands go and encourages Bo to sit. "Why don't we just have you chill there for a bit, huh, buddy?" Nash rustles Bo's hair as my son grabs the cookie from my hand with vigor and is quick to go to town on it.

When Nash and I move to stand, our foreheads bump. "Ow." I rub my head as we part.

Nash chuckles. "Of course, that would happen. We are on the mystical dock."

"The dock." It's barely a whisper from my parted lips.

"Our place."

"Our place," I repeat.

He narrows his eyes at me. "Just going to repeat my words?"

I'm mesmerized because every fiber in my body is aware of what he's about to do. It's my instinct. "That depends."

The gleam in Nash's eyes seems as though he's happy with that answer.

I snicker when he begins to lower to one knee because I knew two minutes ago how this scene would go. It doesn't faze him as he continues his quest, taking hold of my hands and peering up at me.

"Summer." His tone is firm, almost as though he's trying to keep me in line. "You and I have had a long and winding road. Turns out it was leading us to where we should be. Maybe we should have been more then, but we can't change the clock, and here we are now. It's true. I'm supposed to be your last husband."

Tears are beginning to bubble. It's in an odd second, yet right that he references that sentiment from his brother. It doesn't matter because it's true.

"But in order for that to happen, you have to marry me." His sly smirk turns to a fully warm grin.

Now I have to chortle and smile. "I don't hear a question there." No way am I going to make this easy for him.

"You can't question facts." Nash's wink only solidifies my difficulty to ever break this smile.

Lowering to a squat, we come face to face, with my fingertips spread out against his cheeks. "Then it seems we can't challenge that." I love interacting with him this way.

"Exactly," he rasps.

"You know, marrying me comes with some very serious perks." I drop my knees to the dock.

"Oh yeah?" he says, playing along.

I nod once. "Free cookies."

"I partly own this establishment. I already get free cookies."

I tsk him to shut up. "Fine. Remembering the past and being at peace. A great kid."

"Who will have a brother or sister soon."

My eyes widen as my arms link around his neck. "Soon? You might need to wait on that little request."

"What else?"

"Hmm, depends on the ring," I tease him.

"Look in my jeans pocket."

I smirk slyly as my hand dives into the pocket in a way that brings us close, and if we had no audience, then we would probably have clothes off soon. Our lips brush as I slide the ring out of his pocket. Glancing to my side, I hold up the ring. Beautiful and simple. Perfect for me.

I pretend to ponder. "I mean, I guess this works." Nash yanks me closer to kiss my lips, and our teeth touch because our lips are still tightly in a grin. "That list," I murmur against his lips. "You'll also get a wife who will make every shower enjoyable as I will completely be on my knees to take you—" Bo's squeal breaks our attention.

Our foreheads continue to touch as we move to study Bo. "I know, right? Your mommy has such a foul mouth."

Bo holds up his hands with crumbs and icing stuck to his skin. He's grabby because he wants more cookies.

"So, were you in on this too, kid?" I ask my son.

His response in to say, "Mama."

The feeling of my fingers being dragged causes me to look down, and I watch Nash slip the ring on.

"I'm kind of surprised it didn't fall down and between the boards because that's just our style on this dock," he quips.

My hand soars up, and I stretch my fingers to appraise the ring. It's simple, Bohemian, and suits me in every way.

"Not too shabby," I say.

Nash yanks me tight to his body and kisses me with a delicious warning. "You're going to drive me crazy forever, aren't you?"

"And you don't mind."

He swipes a few strands of my hair away, and we get lost in one another's eyes for a few seconds before another kiss is shared between us.

But the clawing at my ankles updates me that someone is getting restless. "Okay, we get the hint. You're happy about this, want more cookies, and you're ready for your car ride to your other uncle." I scoop Bo into my arms and pretend to bite his nose which earns me a few giggles. "You're going to be the cutest little ring bearer, yes you are." My mom voice is out in full.

"Alright, let's get you two in the car. Champagne will have to wait for later because we have a schedule to keep, and you have no sweater on."

I suddenly remember that I have nothing covering my arms, and that causes a shiver from the realization. Then another one runs through my head. "Wait, champagne later? Does Keats know?"

Nash releases a short laugh. "Did you really think I was going to show up at his house with a ring around his sister's finger and face his wrath? Yeah. Yeah, he knows. Seemed neutral about it."

It makes me laugh, as I can only imagine how that conversation went, but then my laugh softens. "And your parents?" Gail never had an issue with Nash and me, and Walter has slowly come around.

Nash touches my shoulder to put me at ease. "They're fine." My smile begins to etch on my lips again.

"Let's go then. Seems everything is in place."

"It is."

Our delicate voices and our eyes catching are the perfect confirmation that we are exactly where we should be. Where we always should have been.

———

THE CAR RIDE was needed to gather my strength for balancing the testosterone between Keats and Nash. As he drives, we've been sharing pure puppy eyes and giddy looks. We're nearly over the top, and I'm sure it will make my brother scowl a few times.

"Here we are." Nash sighs as we turn onto my brother's street.

I chuckle. "Enthusiasm to the brim," I retort.

"Don't get me wrong. It's just… we haven't really stayed in a family member's house since we've been together. I'm not sure Keats should be our trial." We decided to stay overnight, makes it easier if we want to enjoy wine.

I rub his hand where it's sitting on the middle console. I find this entertaining. "We'll be fine. Besides, I think he still has work to do, and it will be just a chill dinner. A BBQ maybe."

Nash's eyes seem focused through the front window of the car as he slows down. When he tilts his head and eyes squint, it causes me to wonder what's happening. "Uh, looks like your brother is going to be *on* a BBQ."

My eyes snap forward as we come to a stop in front of his

house. He's in the front yard with a woman our age arguing with him, and Keats seems to be dishing it right back.

Hesitantly, I unbuckle my belt and open the door to hop out. They seem unaware of our arrival.

"You. You are the one who dragged me to that party," she seethes.

"Really, Esme? Pretty positive you got an invite too, and it just so happens we ended up driving home together."

She points a finger at my brother. "You are the worst neighbor. You are such a mind fuck."

I stand there in awe and feel Nash arrive by my side. I'm not sure either of us blink, too engrossed in the scene.

"Do we interrupt them, let them know to tone down the language before I take Bo out?" Nash wonders.

"I'm not sure. I kind of want to see how this plays out."

Nash's eyes and my own nearly pop out when my brother steps forward and so does Esme. Ah, I know this scene. A reminder of Nash and I pre-reunion, which is why I smirk.

"It's not my fault you voluntarily came home with me and then we—"

"Whoa," I speak up and wave my hand. "We don't need to hear more."

Both Keats and Esme whip their sight to us, suddenly aware of our presence.

Nash just smirks, clearly enjoying my brother's shock or embarrassment, I'm not sure what it is.

"How long have you been standing there?" Keats asks, frozen.

"Long enough for me to enjoy this weekend's *roasted* BBQ." Nash has a cheeky smile—because he won't let this go—right before he turns to open Bo's door with vigor.

My fingers give a little wiggle wave. "You must be the neighbor. I've heard about you. Not exactly in your favor," I admit with a tight smile. "But you seem to be handling my brother… kind of… maybe."

"Summer," Keats grits out a warning.

"What?' My voice rises an octave as I shrug. "Clearly she returns the sentiment, and it's not my problem that we showed up to your lovers' quarrel."

"We are not lovers," they both say in unison.

Nash just chuckles under his breath. "Sure, you aren't."

What an eventful dinner this is going to be.

9 781959 094418